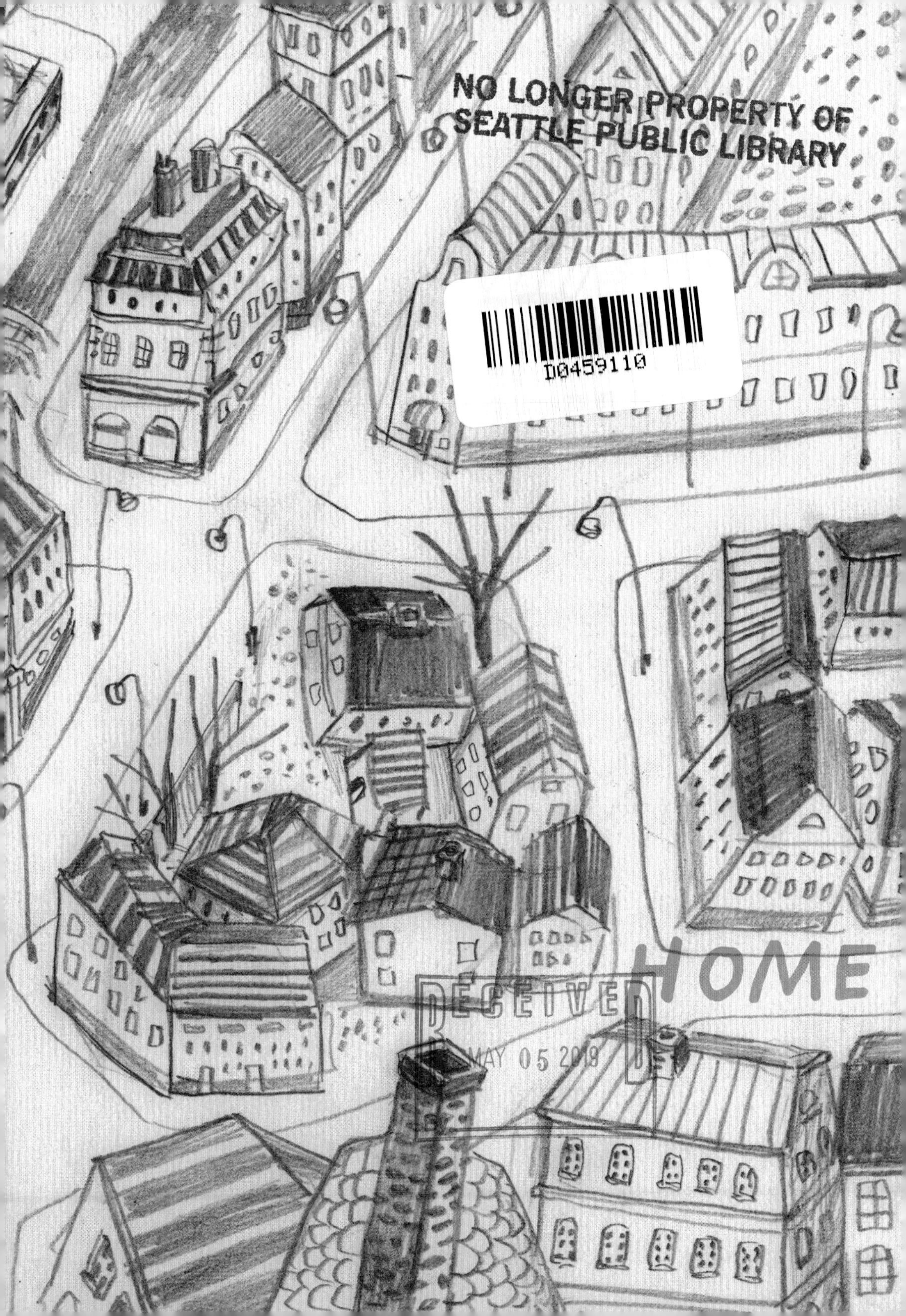
HOME

Din tur, Adrian
Copyright © Helena Öberg (text), Kristin Lidström (illustrations)
and Mirando Bok, Stockholm, 2015
Published in agreement with Koja Agency
English translation copyright © 2019 by Eva Apelqvist

First published in Swedish in 2015 by Bokförlaget Mirando,
Stockholm, Sweden
Published in English in Canada and the USA in 2019
by Groundwood Books, in agreement with Koja Agency

Groundwood Books / House of Anansi Press
groundwoodbooks.com

We gratefully acknowledge the Government of Canada for its
financial support of our publishing program.

With the participation of the Government of Canada
Avec la participation du gouvernement du Canada | Canadä

Library and Archives Canada Cataloguing in Publication
Öberg, Helena
[Din tur, Adrian. English]
Your turn, Adrian / Helena Öberg ; Kristin Lidström, illustrator;
translated by Eva Apelqvist.
Translation of: Din tur, Adrian.
First published in Swedish in 2015.
Issued in print and electronic formats.
ISBN 978-1-77306-149-8 (hardcover).—ISBN 978-1-77306-150-4 (PDF)
1. Graphic novels. I. Lidström, Kristin, illustrator II. Apelqvist,
Eva, translator III. Title. IV. Title: Din tur, Adrian. English.
PN6790.S88D5613 2019   j741.5'9485   C2018-903430-0
C2018-903431-9

The black-and-white illustrations were hand drawn in pencil;
the color illustrations were done in gouache and ink,
with additions in Photoshop.
Printed and bound in Malaysia

YOUR TURN, ADRIAN

HELENA ÖBERG
KRISTIN LIDSTRÖM

Translated by Eva Apelqvist

GROUNDWOOD BOOKS
HOUSE OF ANANSI PRESS
Toronto Berkeley

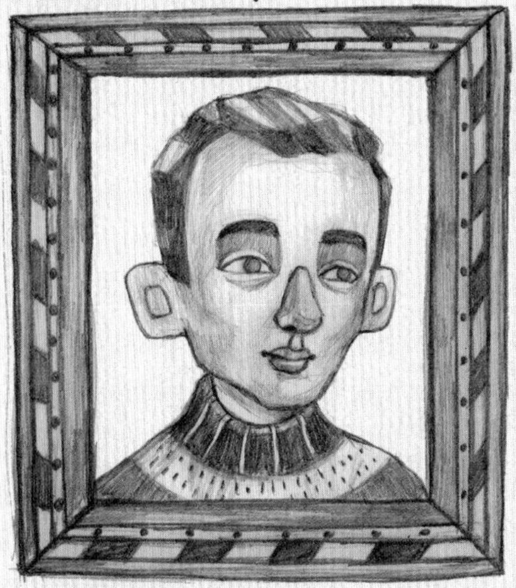
Adrian

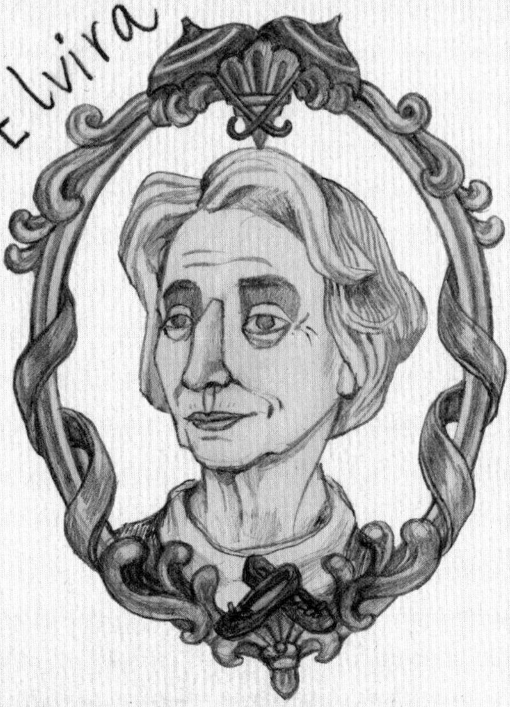
Elvira

2 HEIDI

page 28

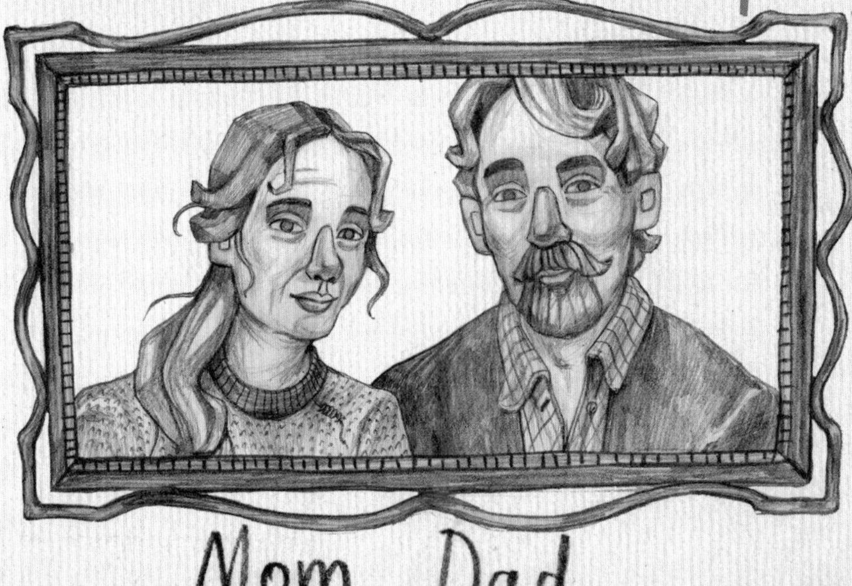
Mom
Dad

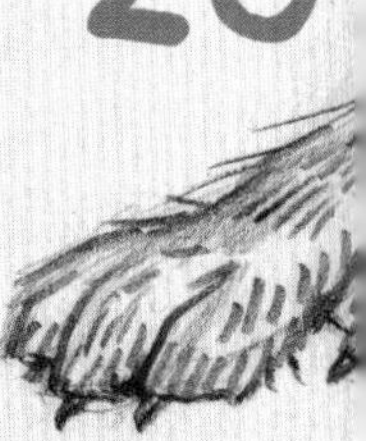

BEFORE I MET

Heidi

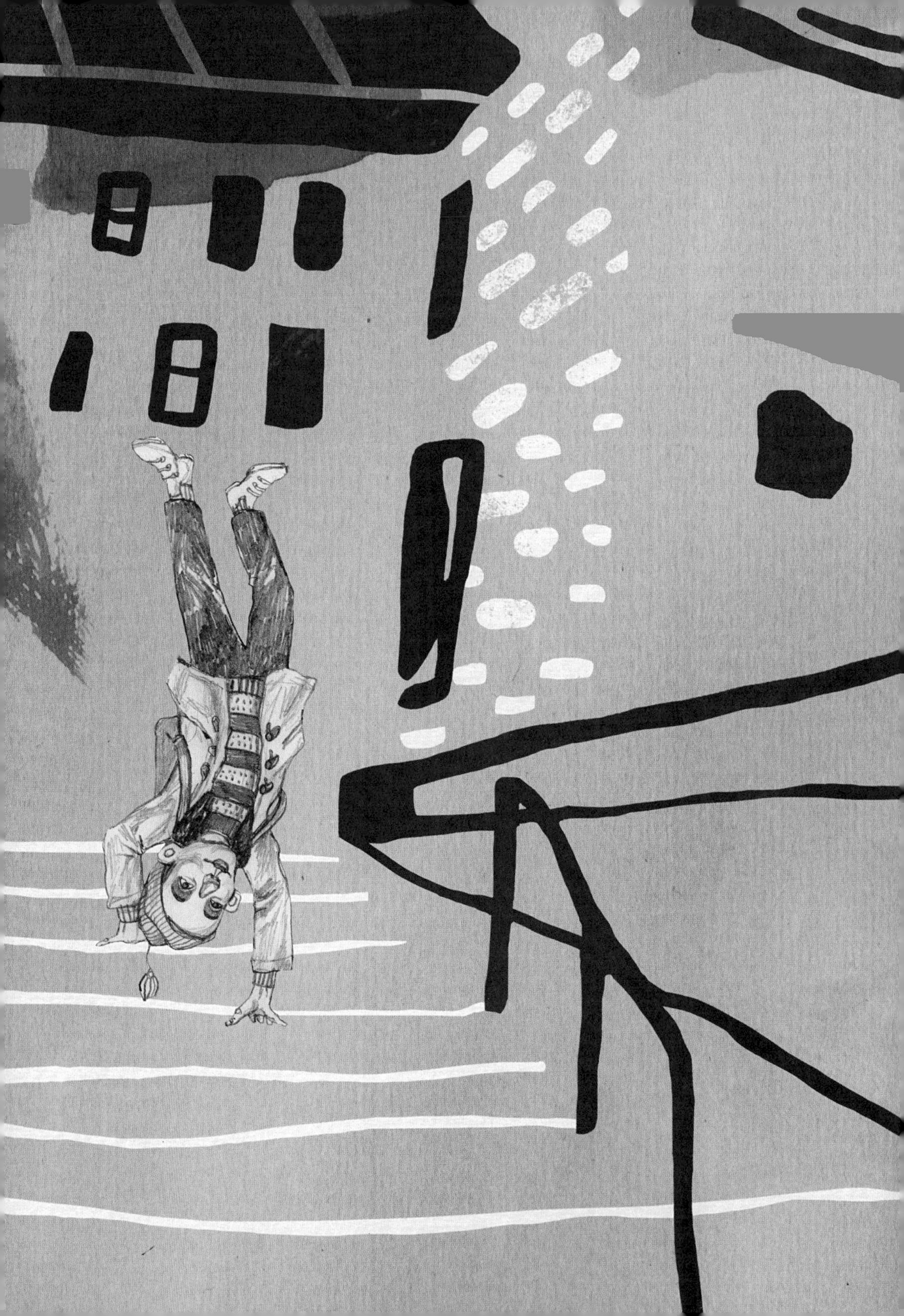

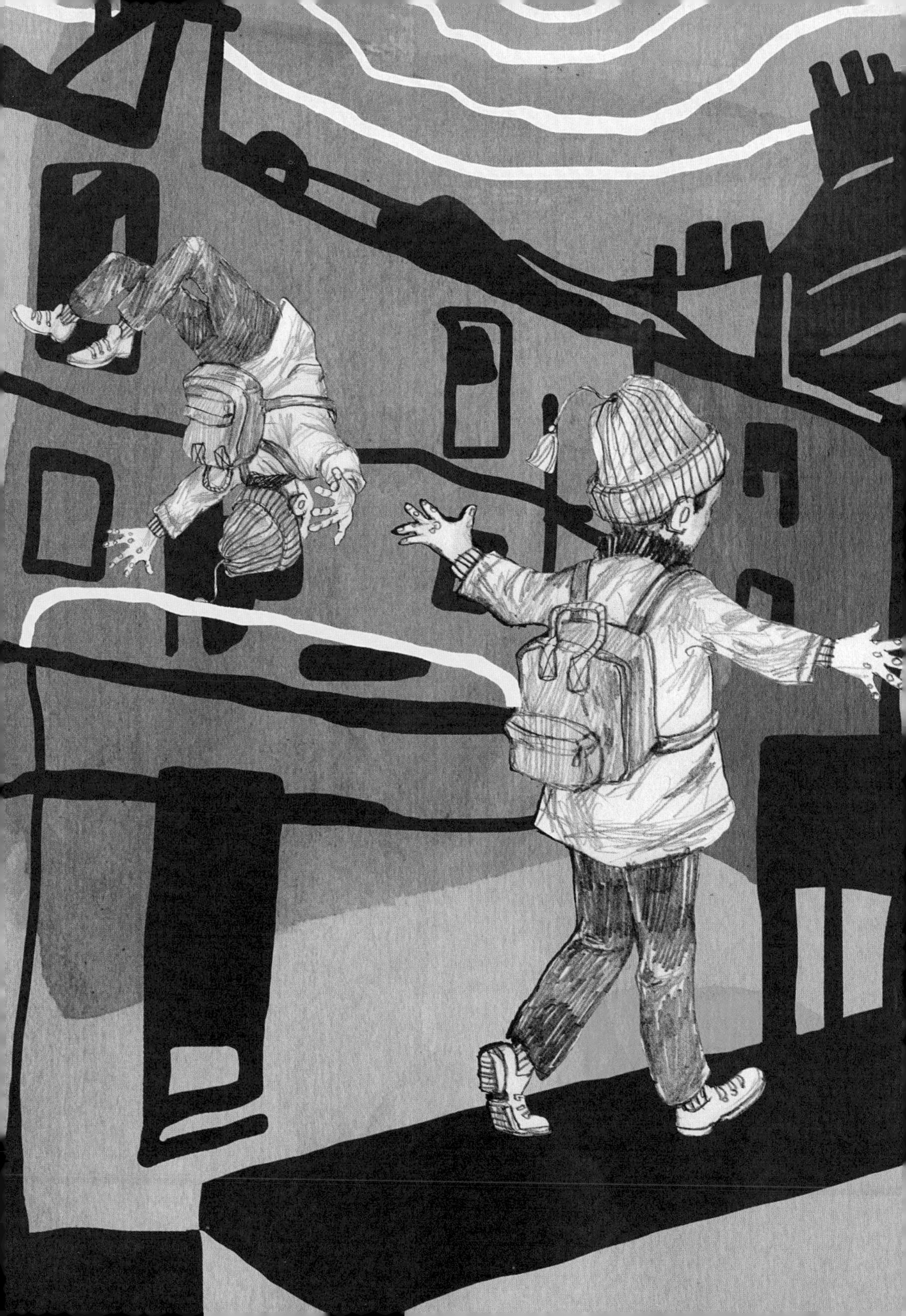

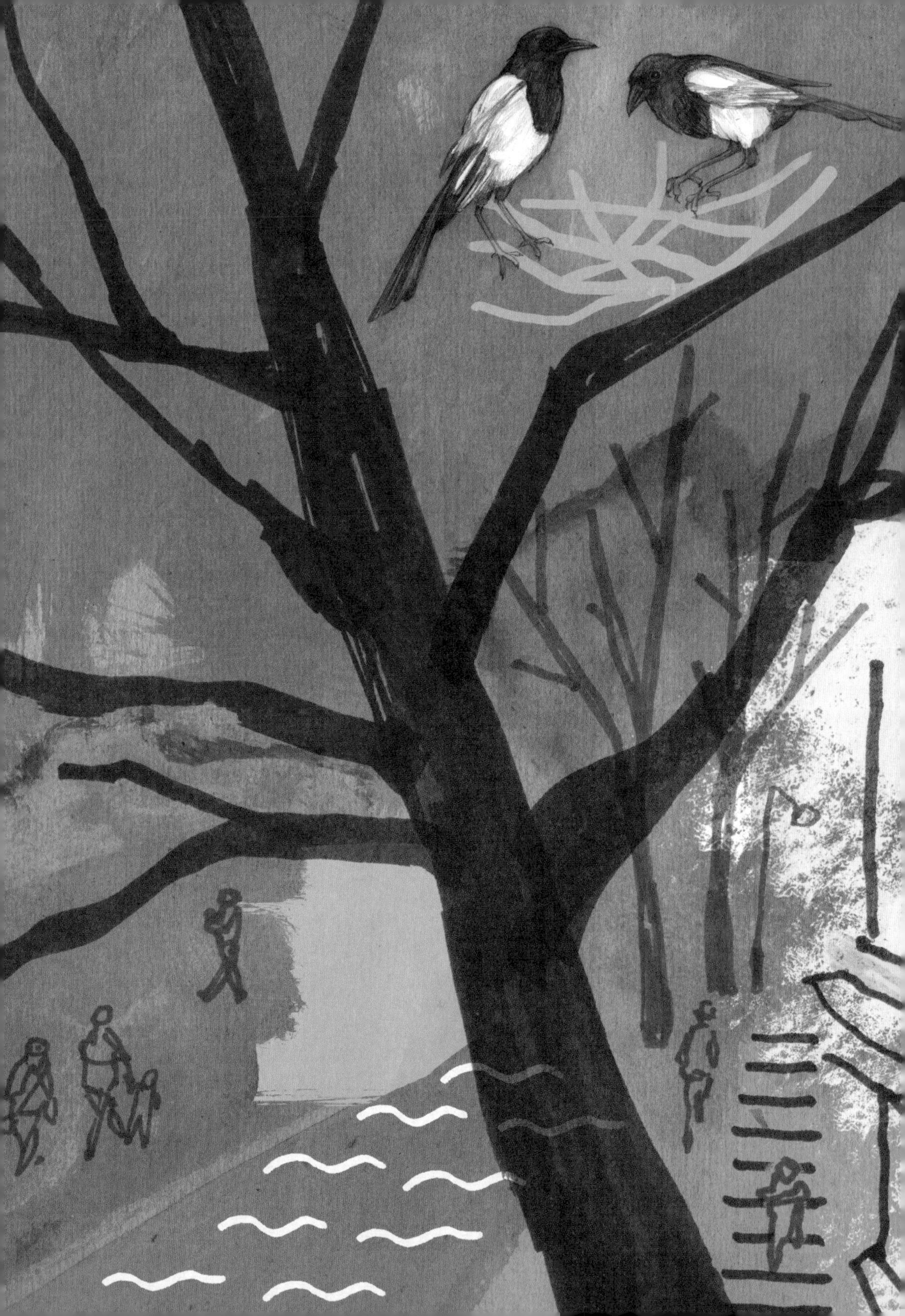

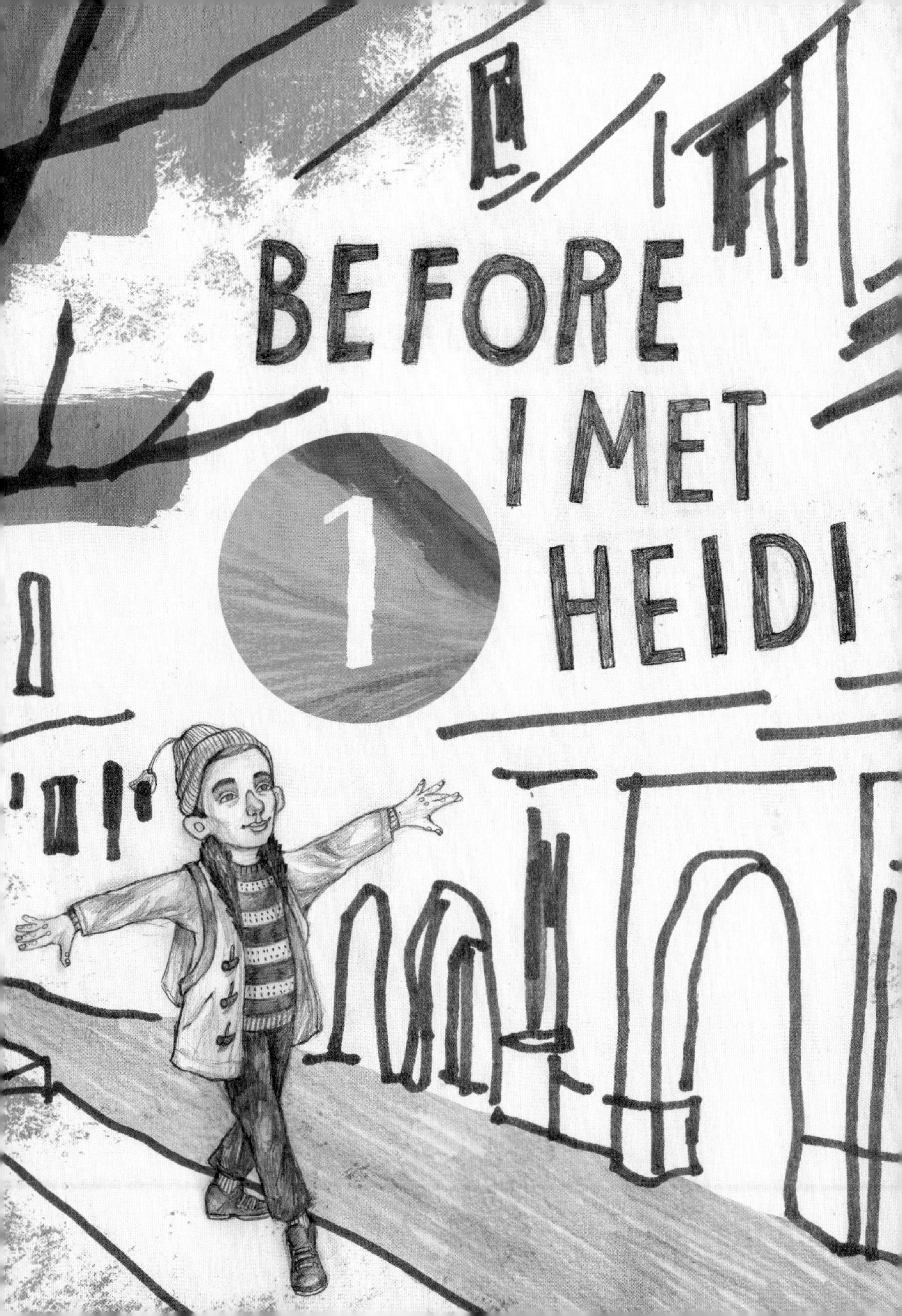
BEFORE I MET HEIDI
1

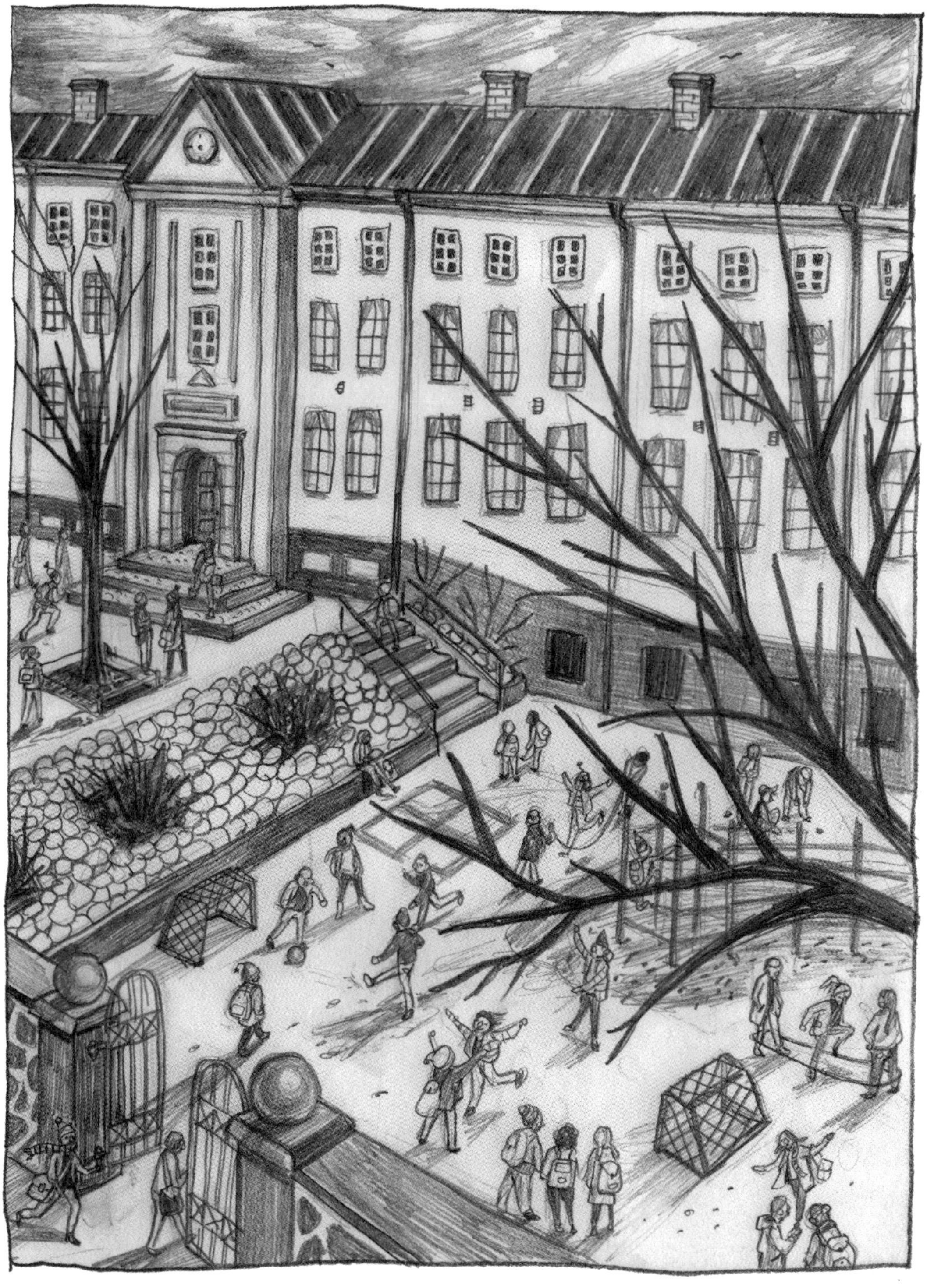

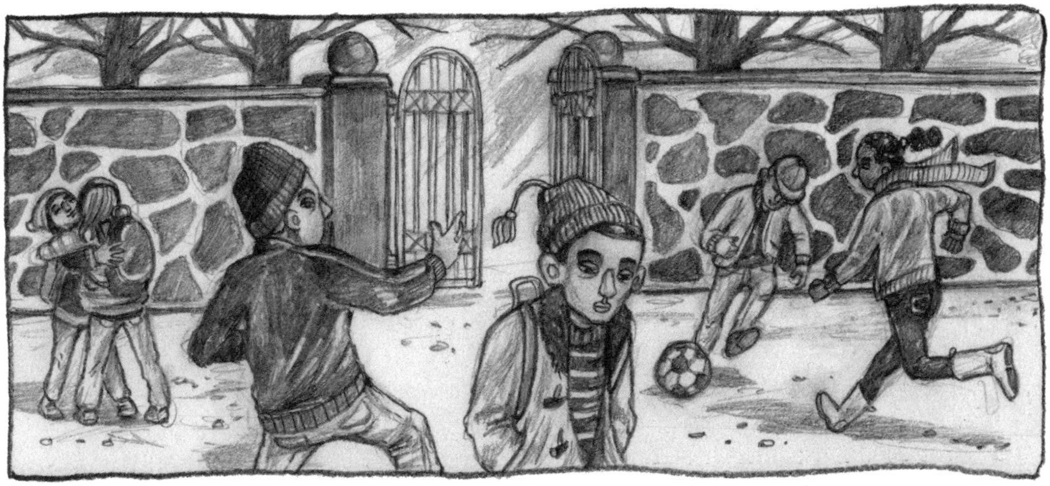

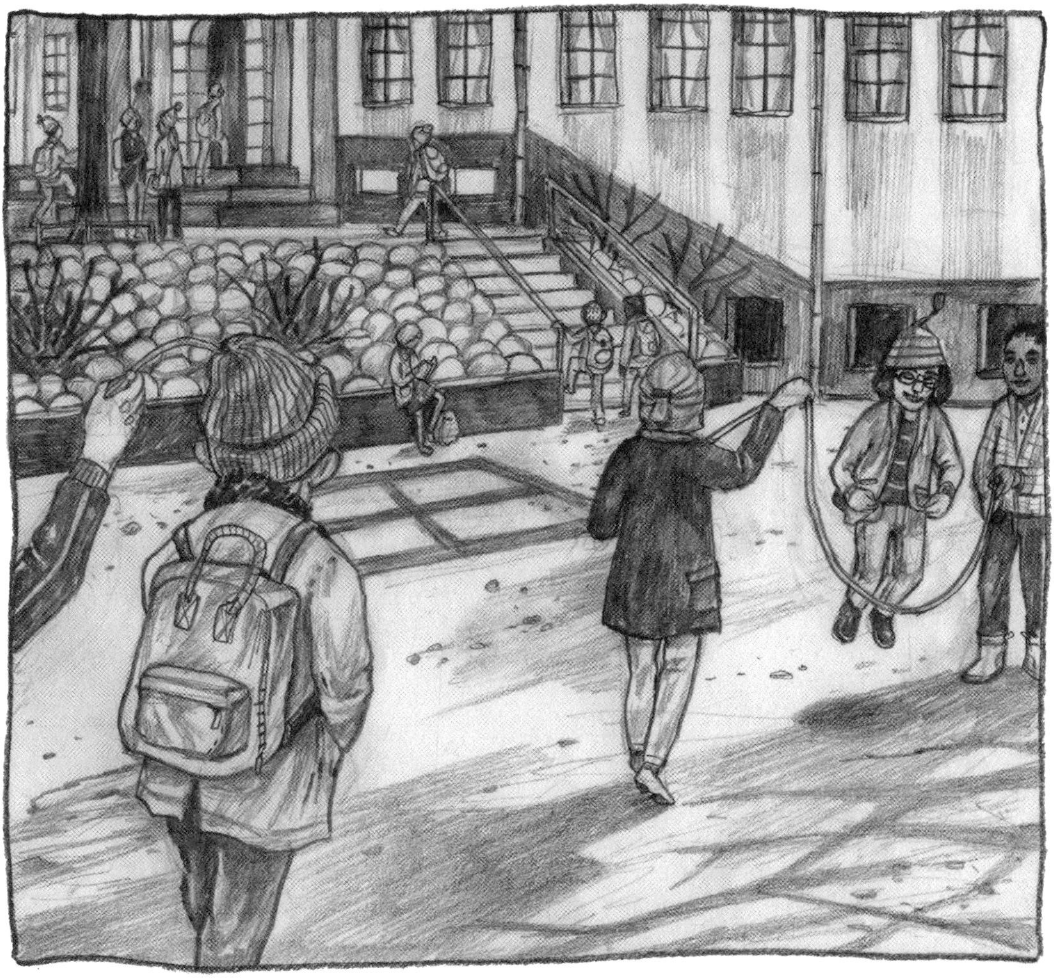

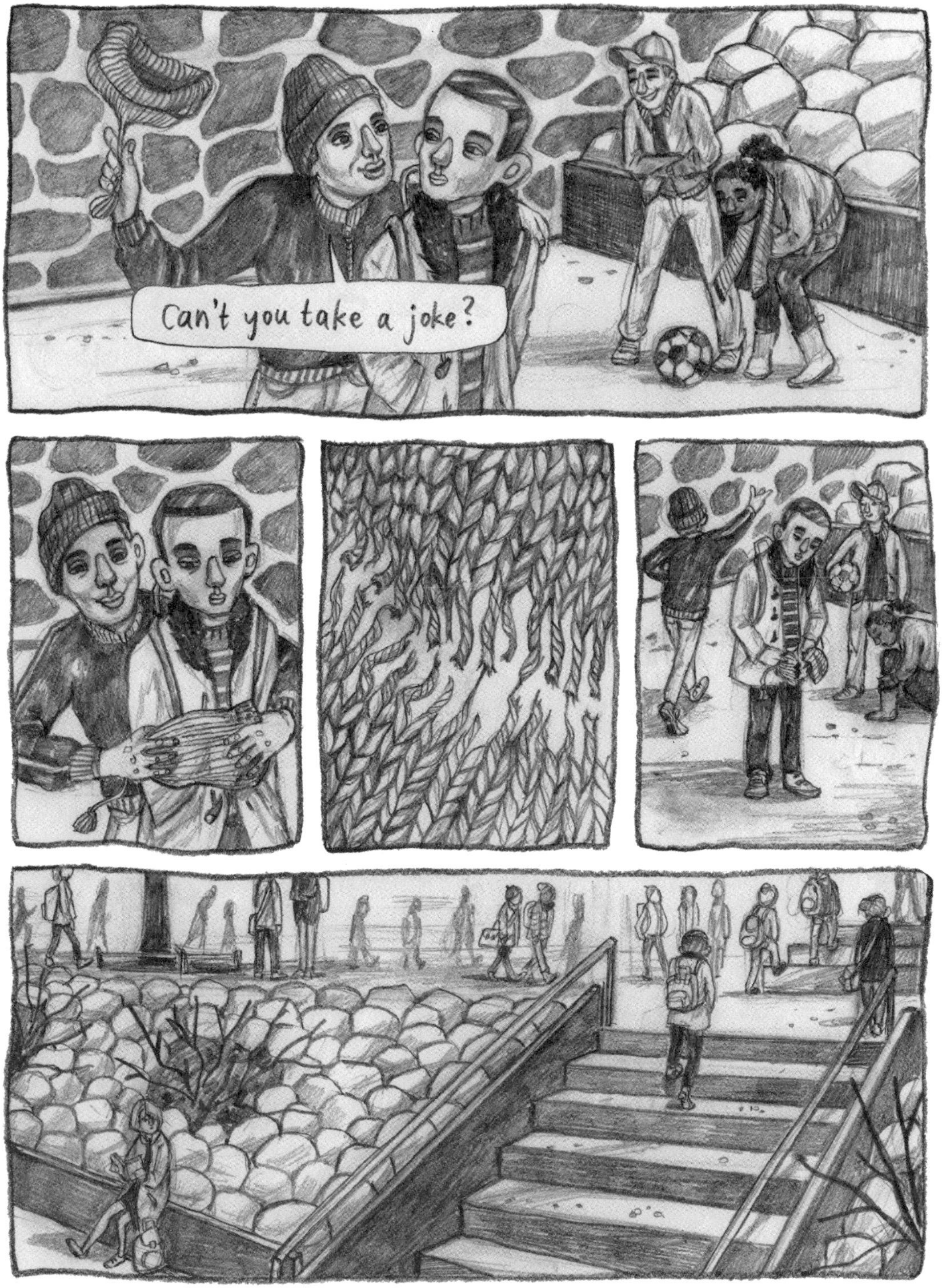
Can't you take a joke?

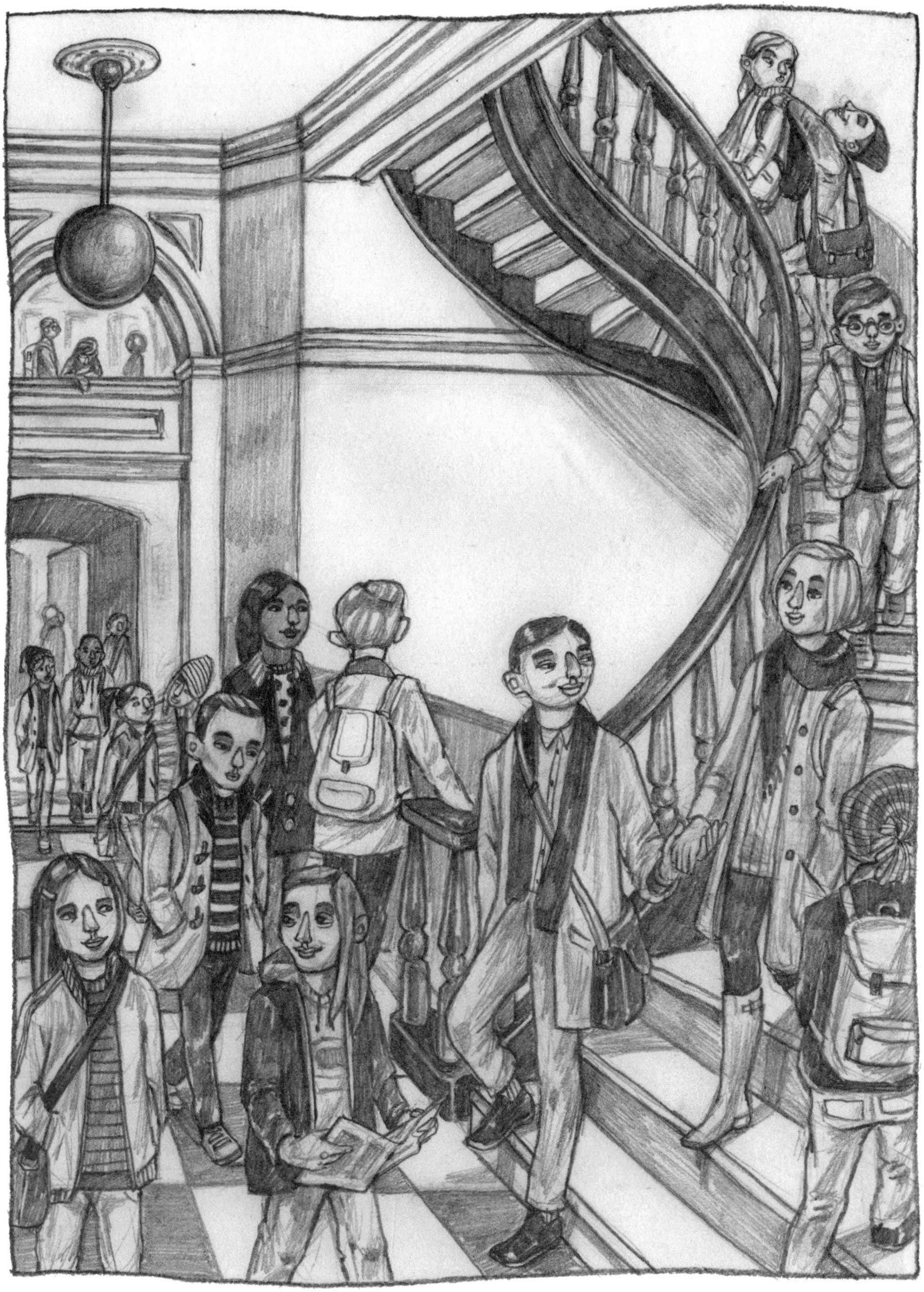

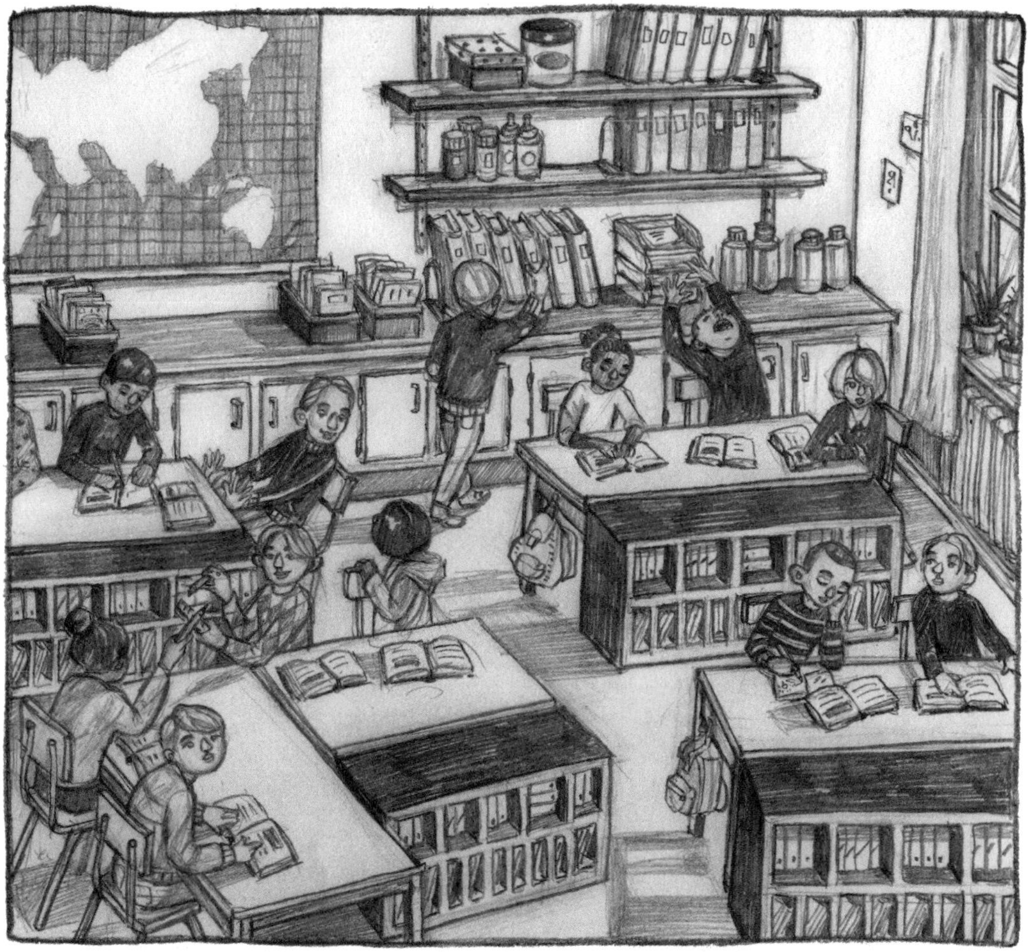

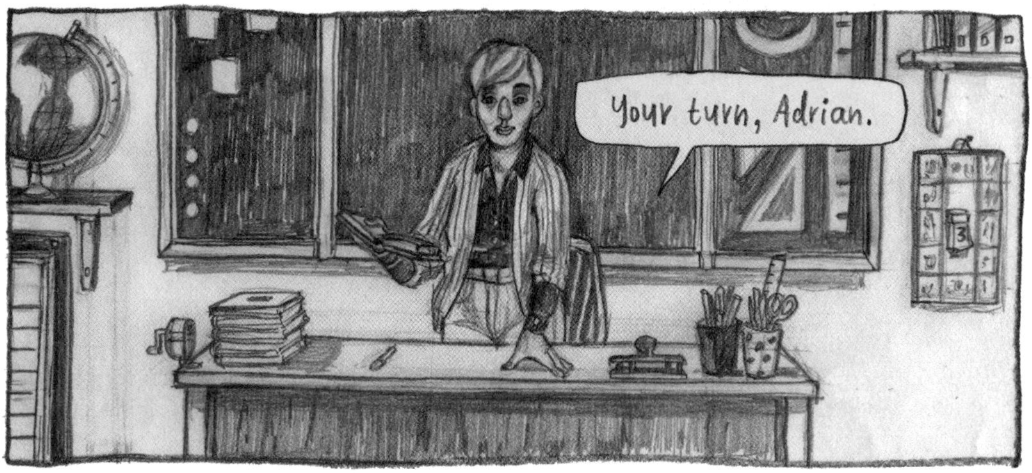
Your turn, Adrian.

Sometimes the teacher asked me a question.

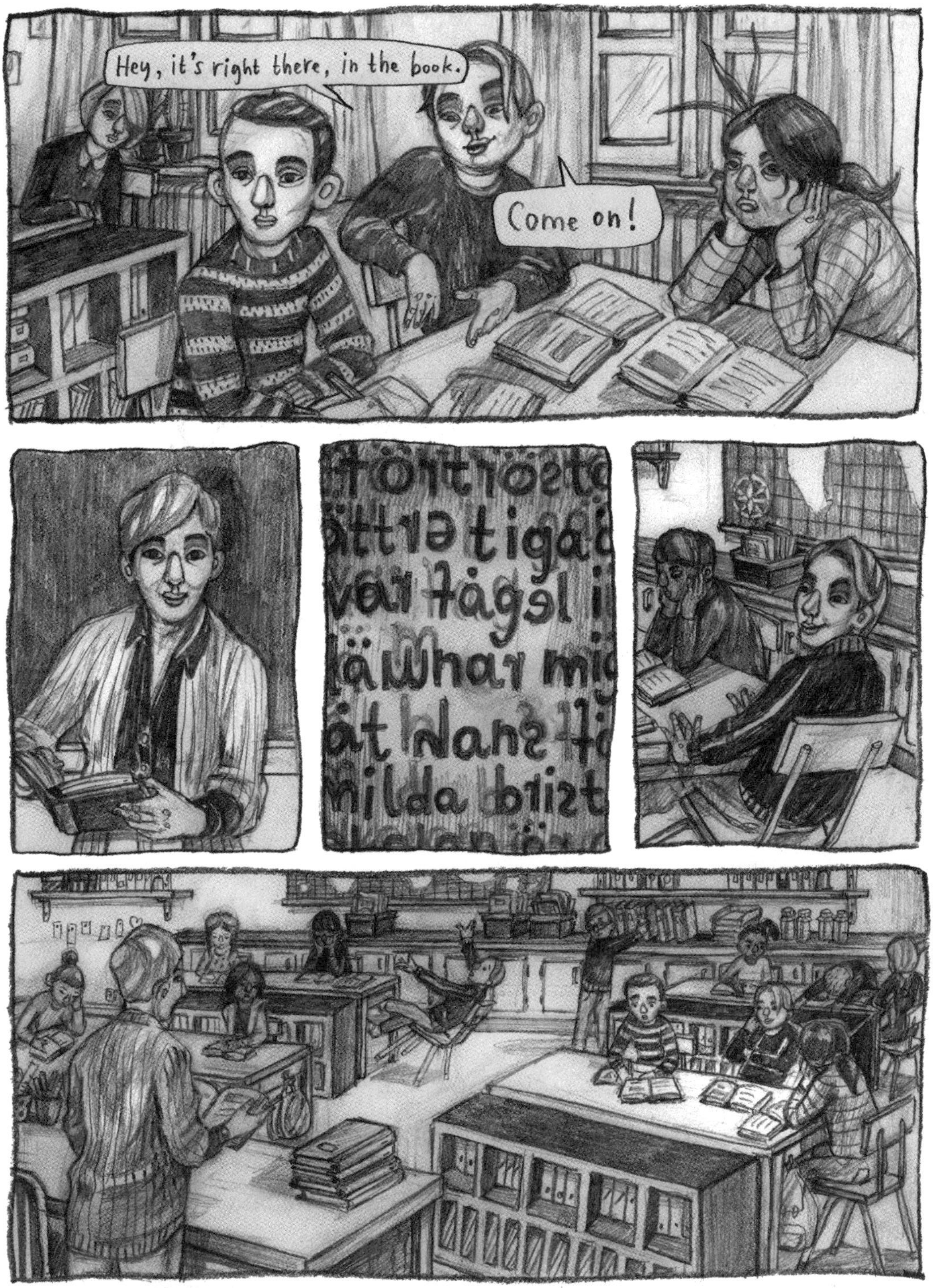
Hey, it's right there, in the book.
Come on!

My heart was pounding. My head was in a fog.

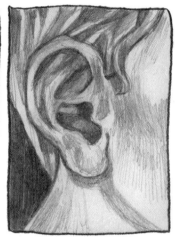

My cheeks burned.

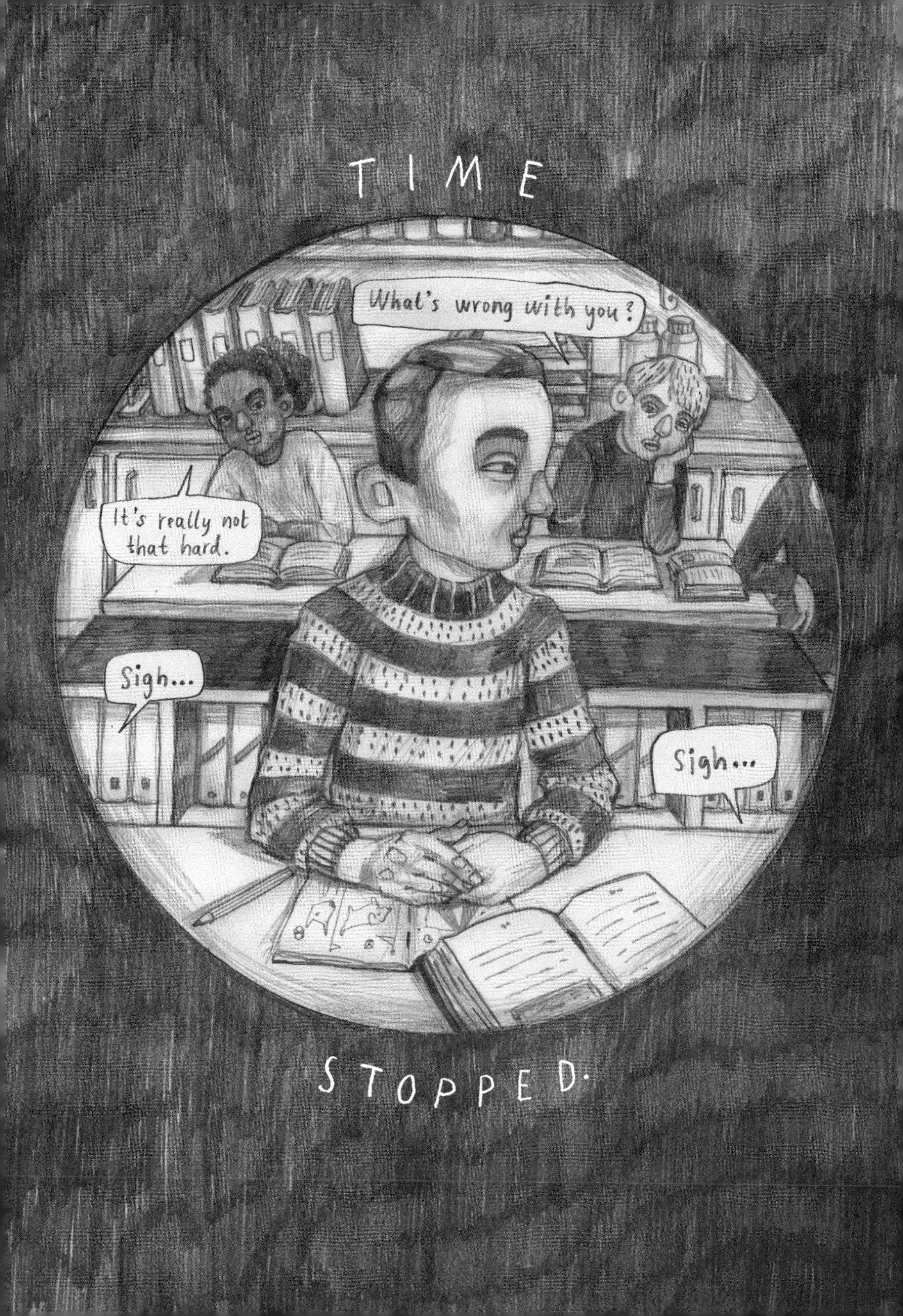
TIME
What's wrong with you?
It's really not that hard.
Sigh...
Sigh...
STOPPED.

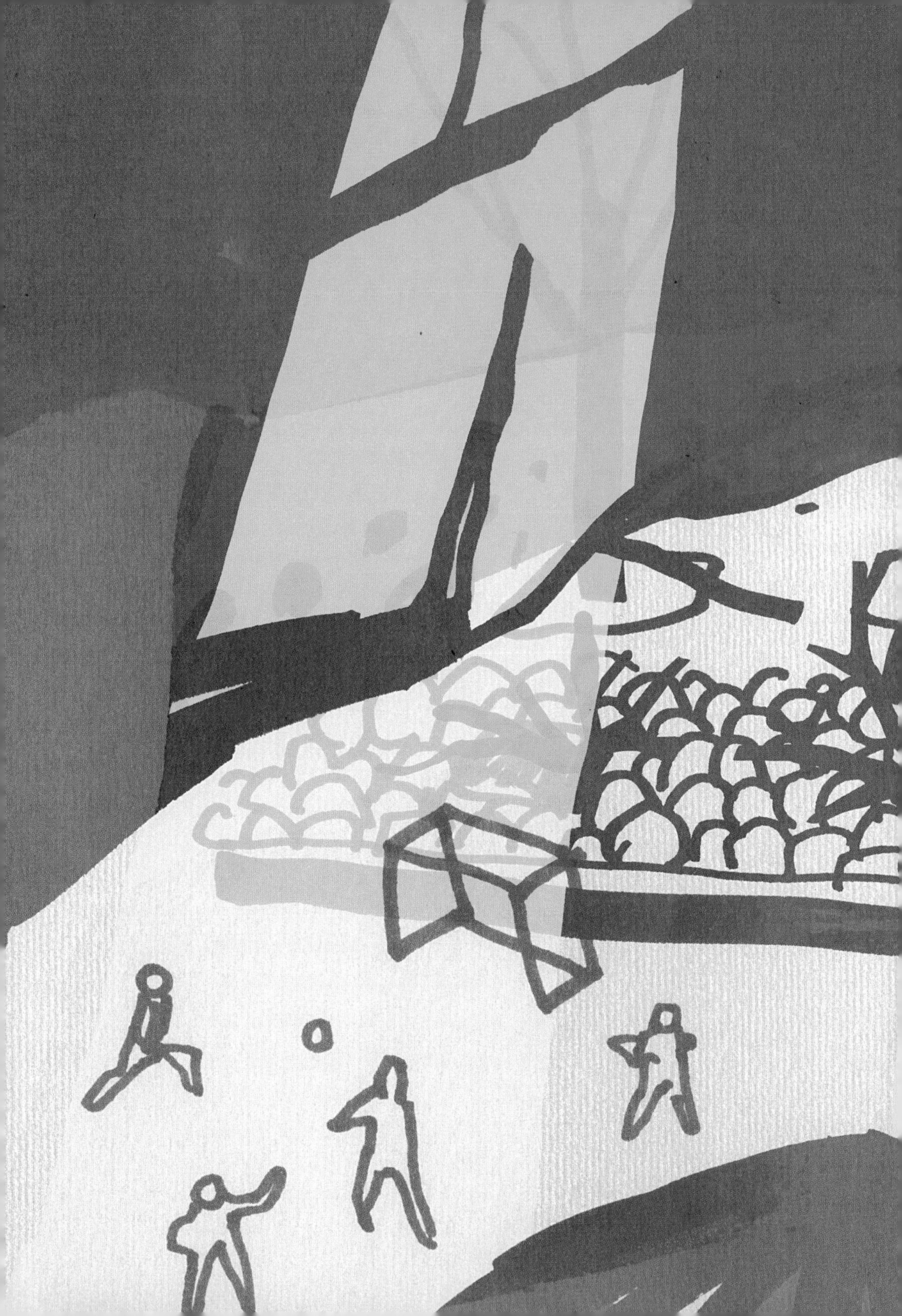

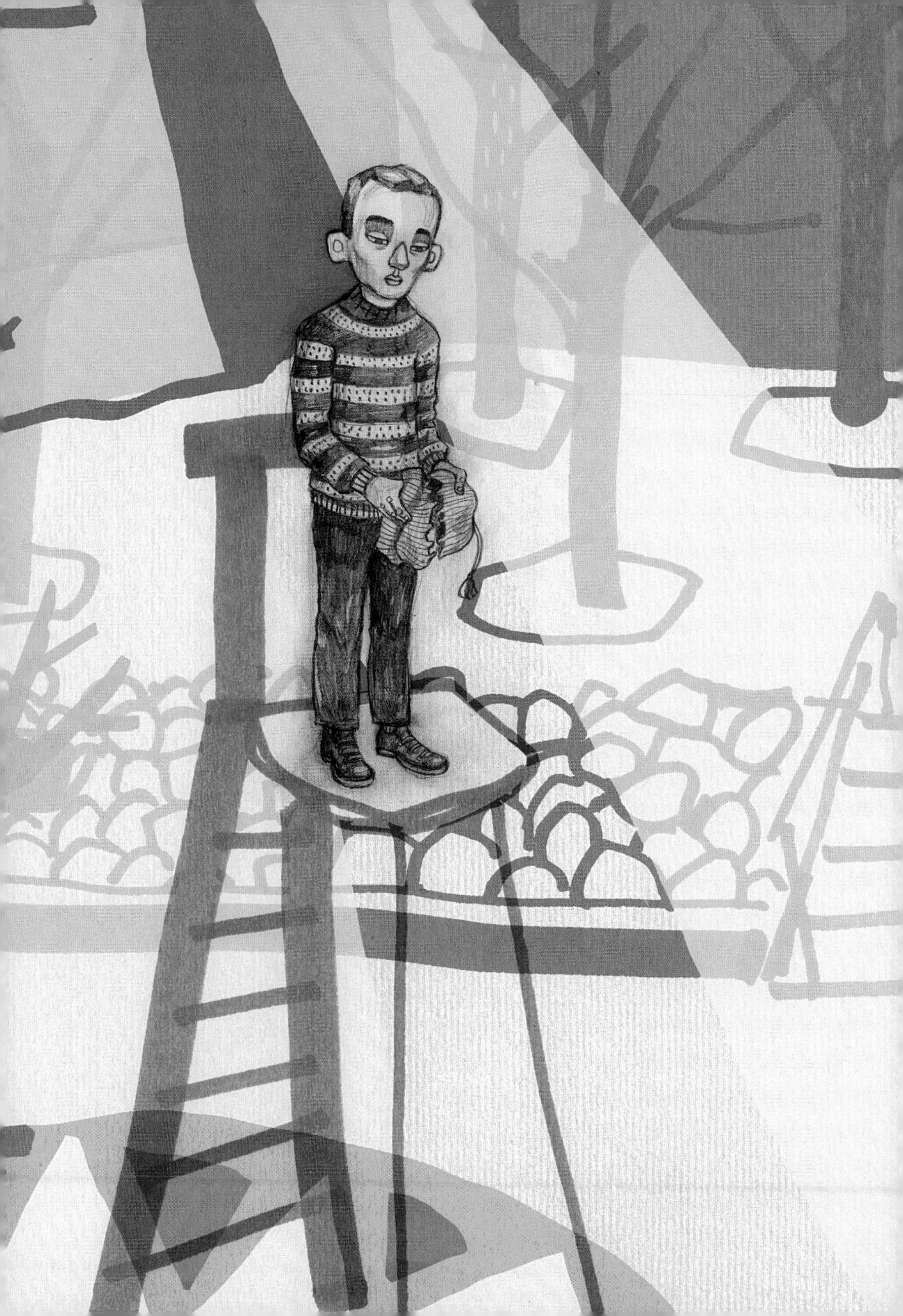

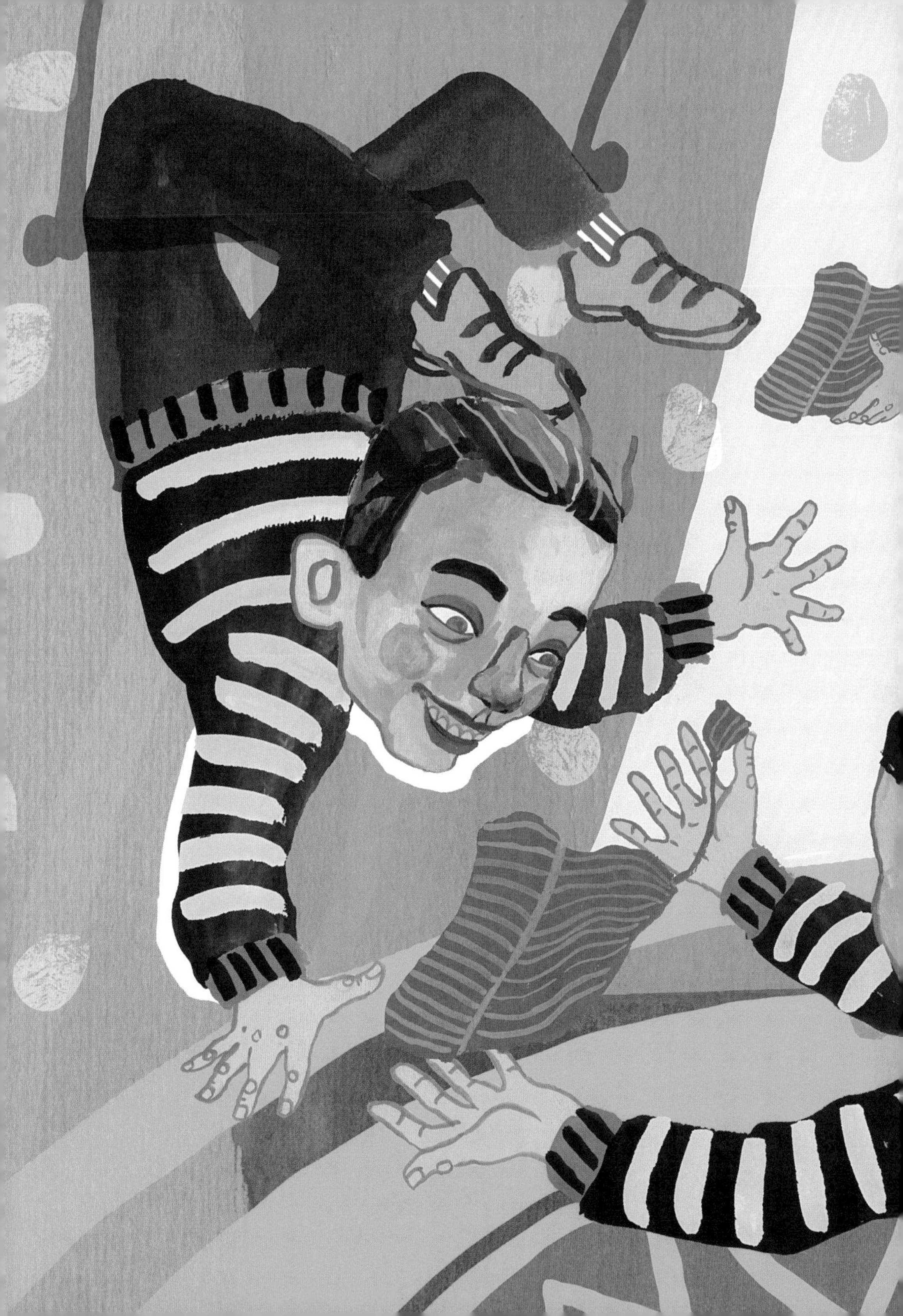

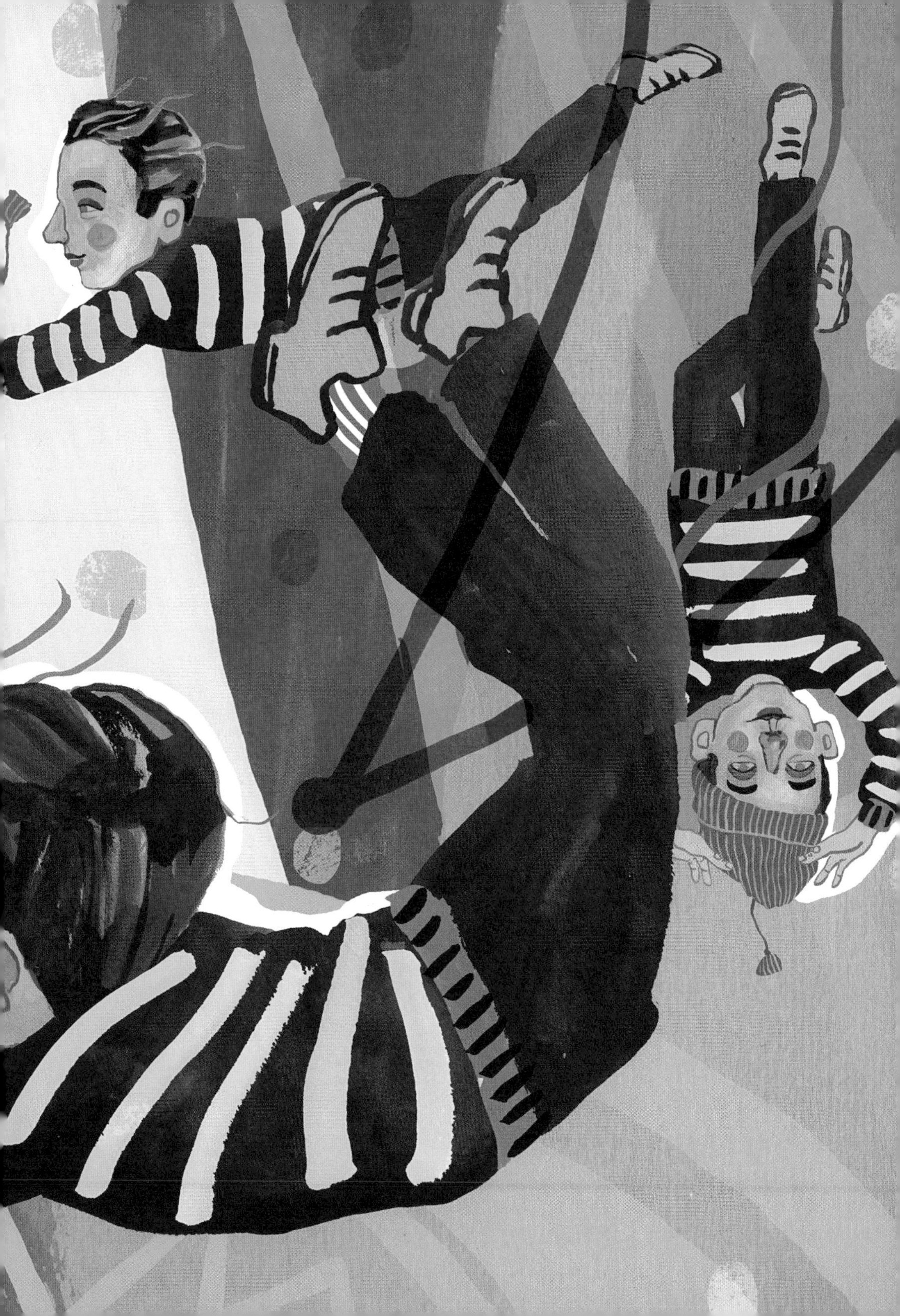

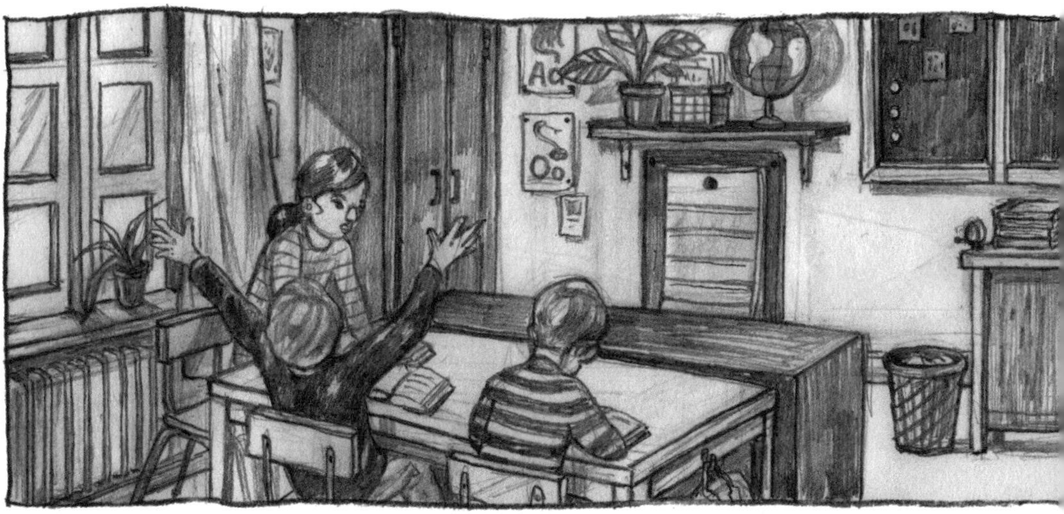

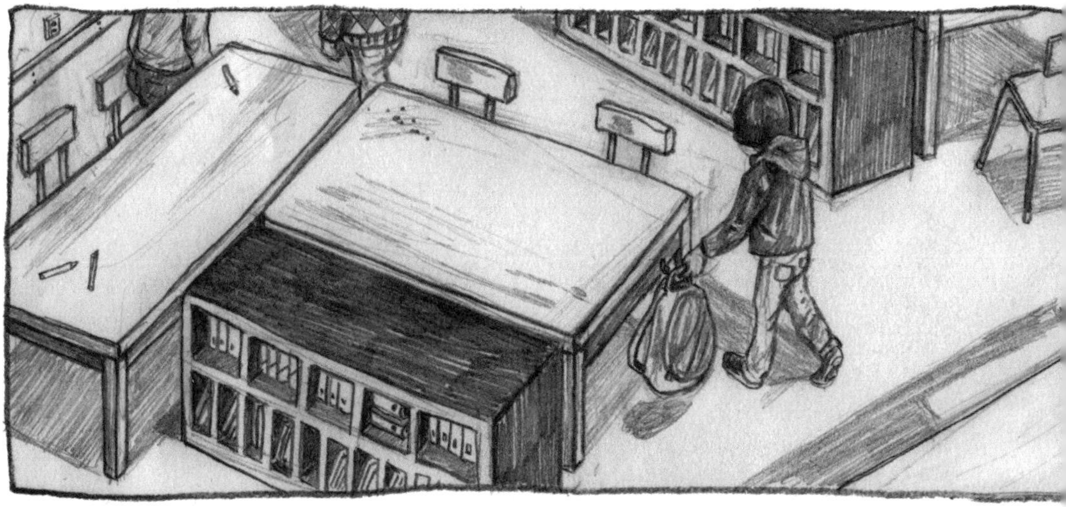

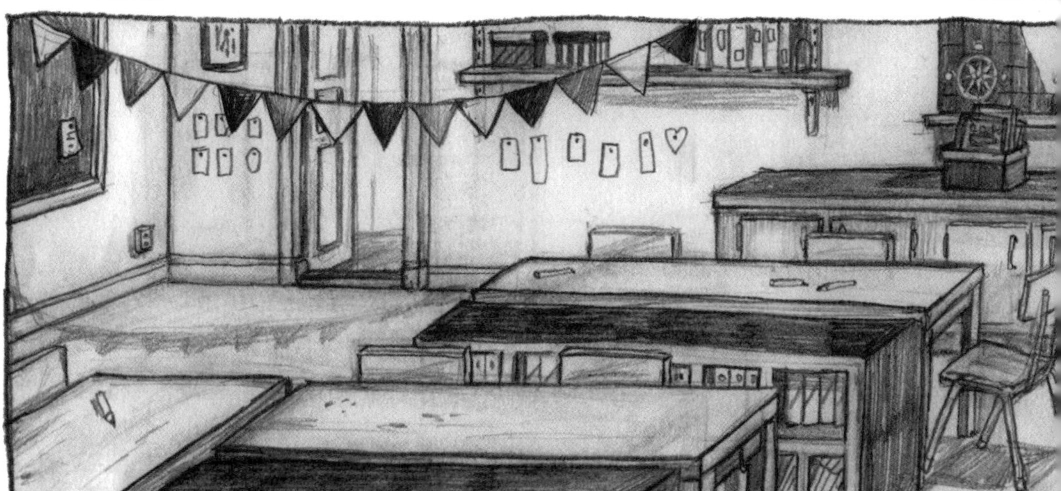

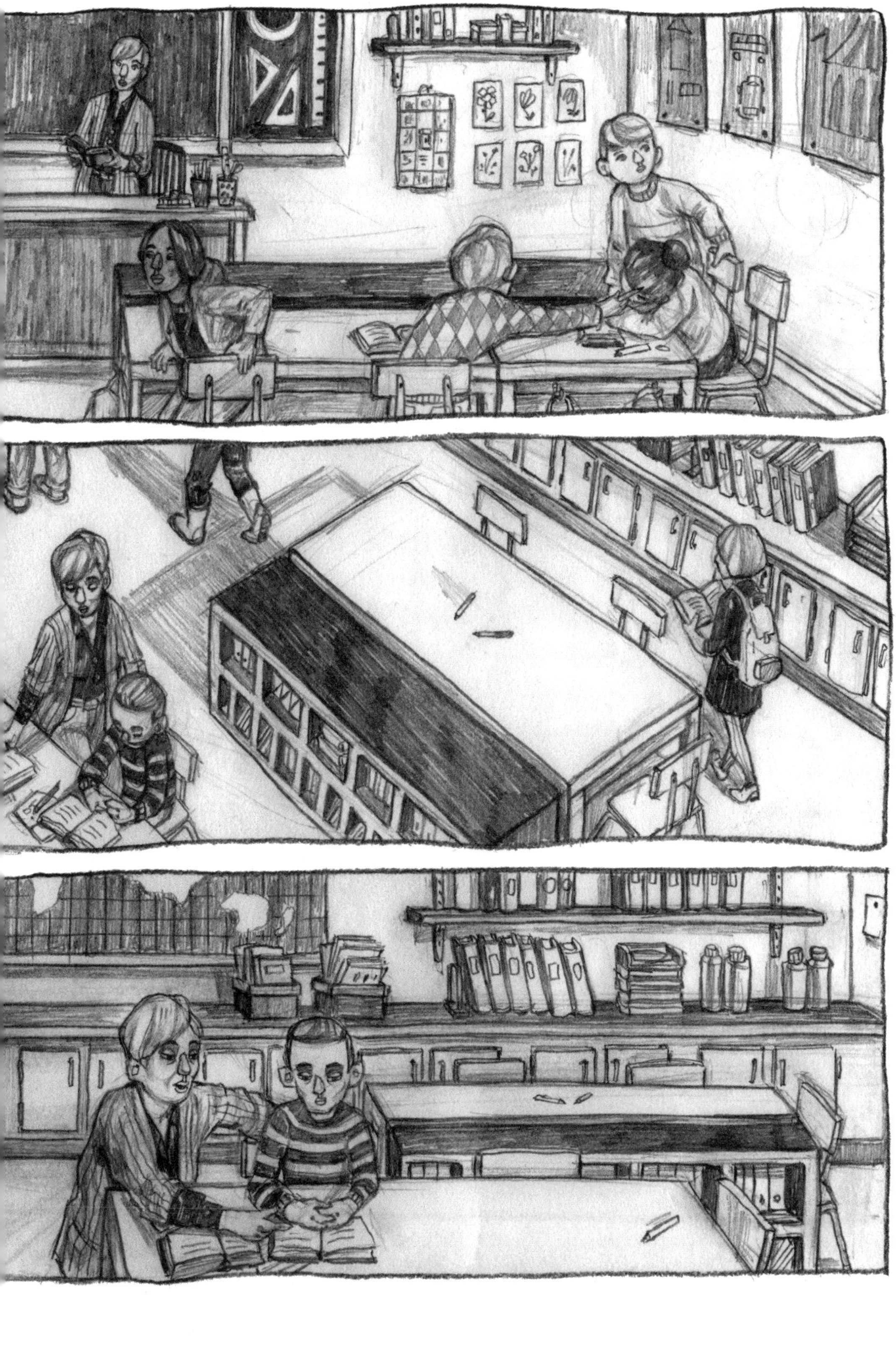

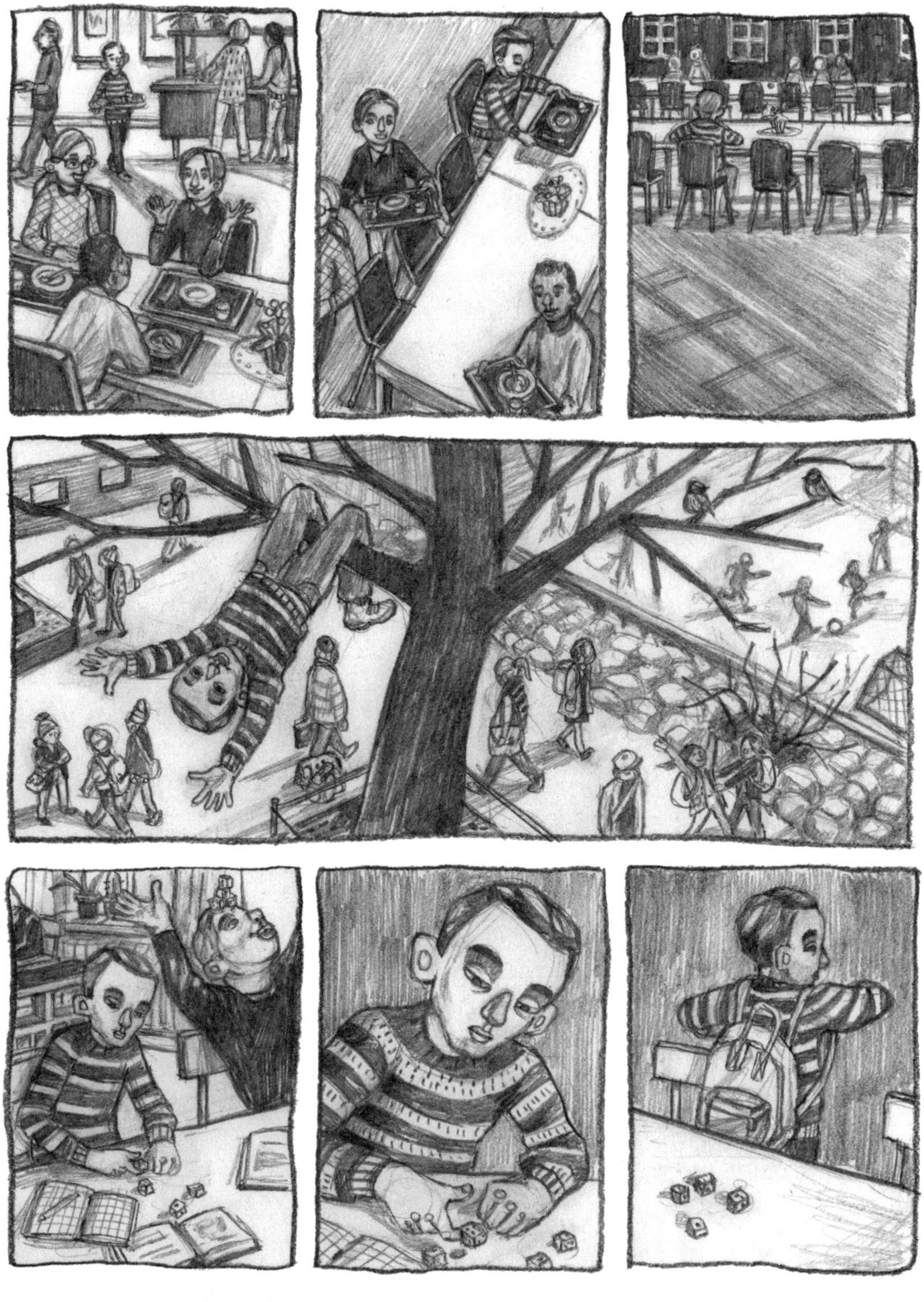

When the bell rang, I went home.

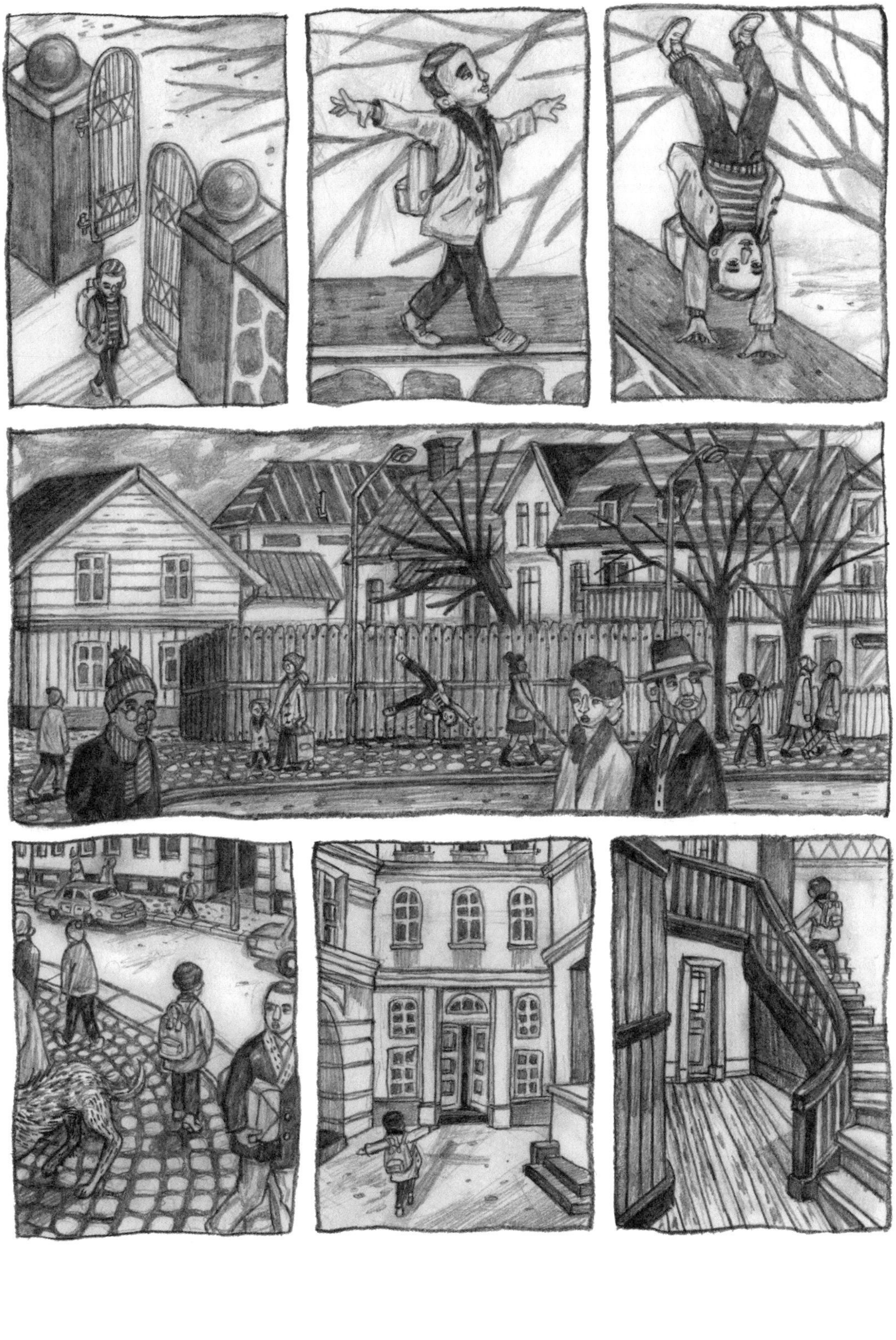

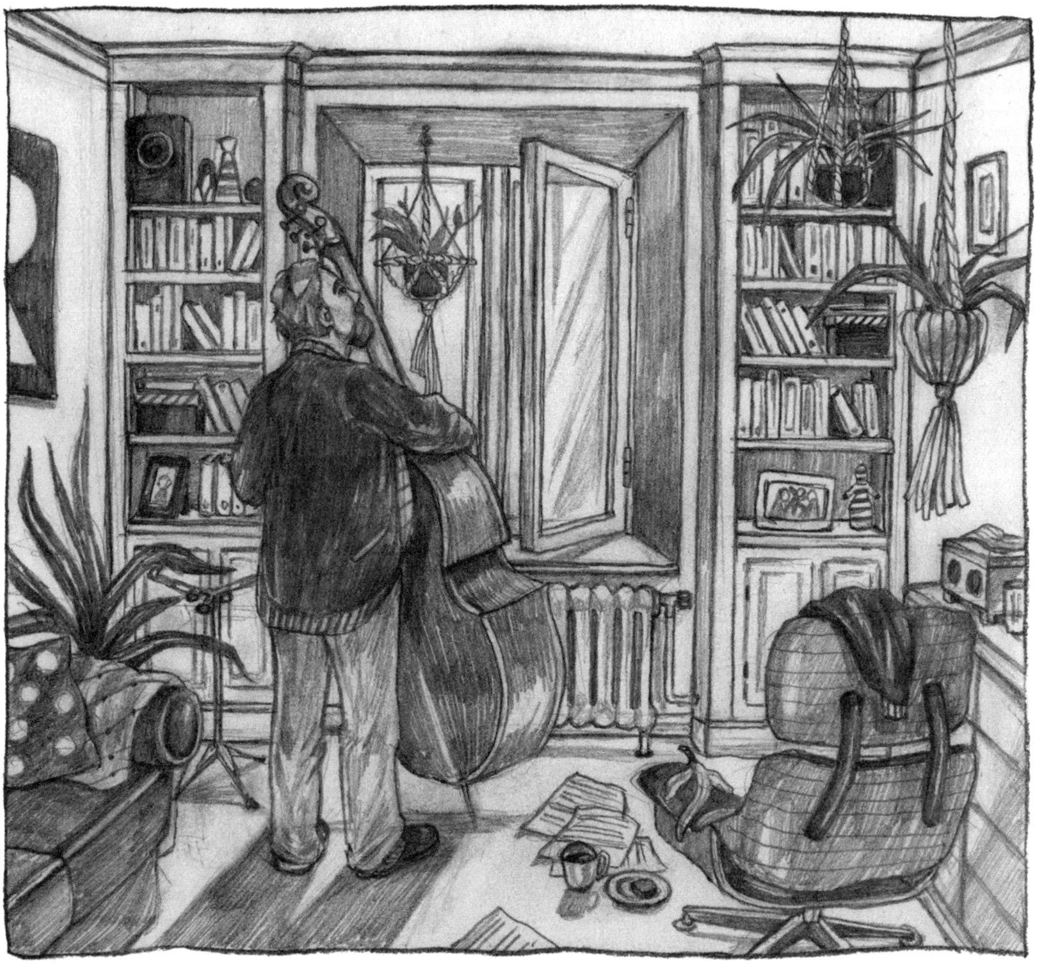

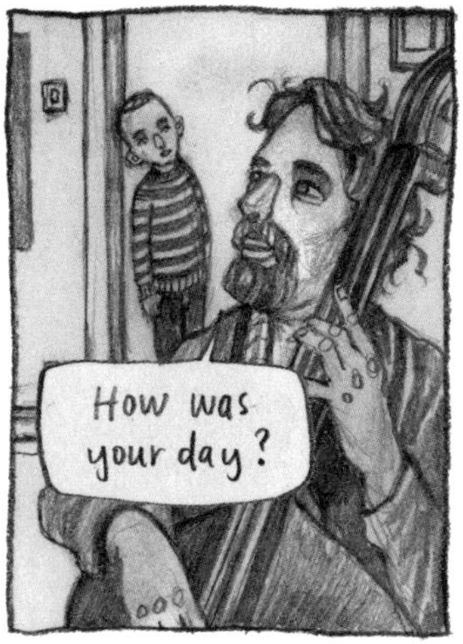
How was your day?

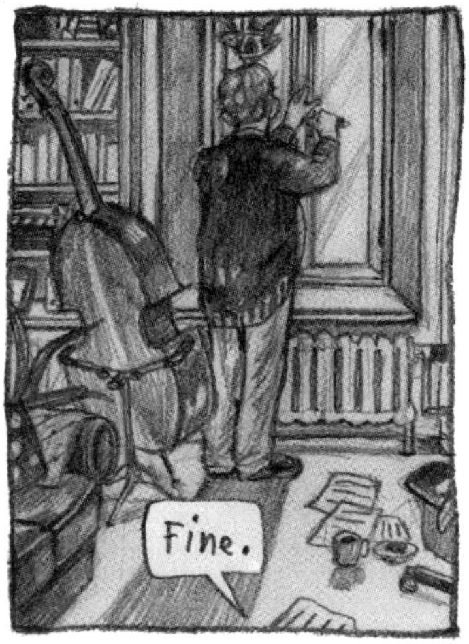
Fine.

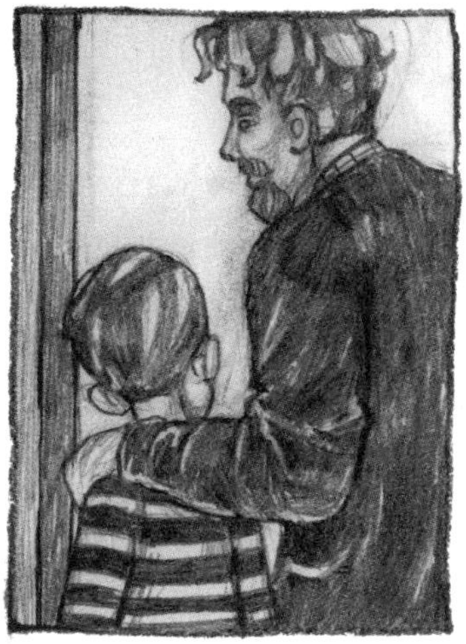

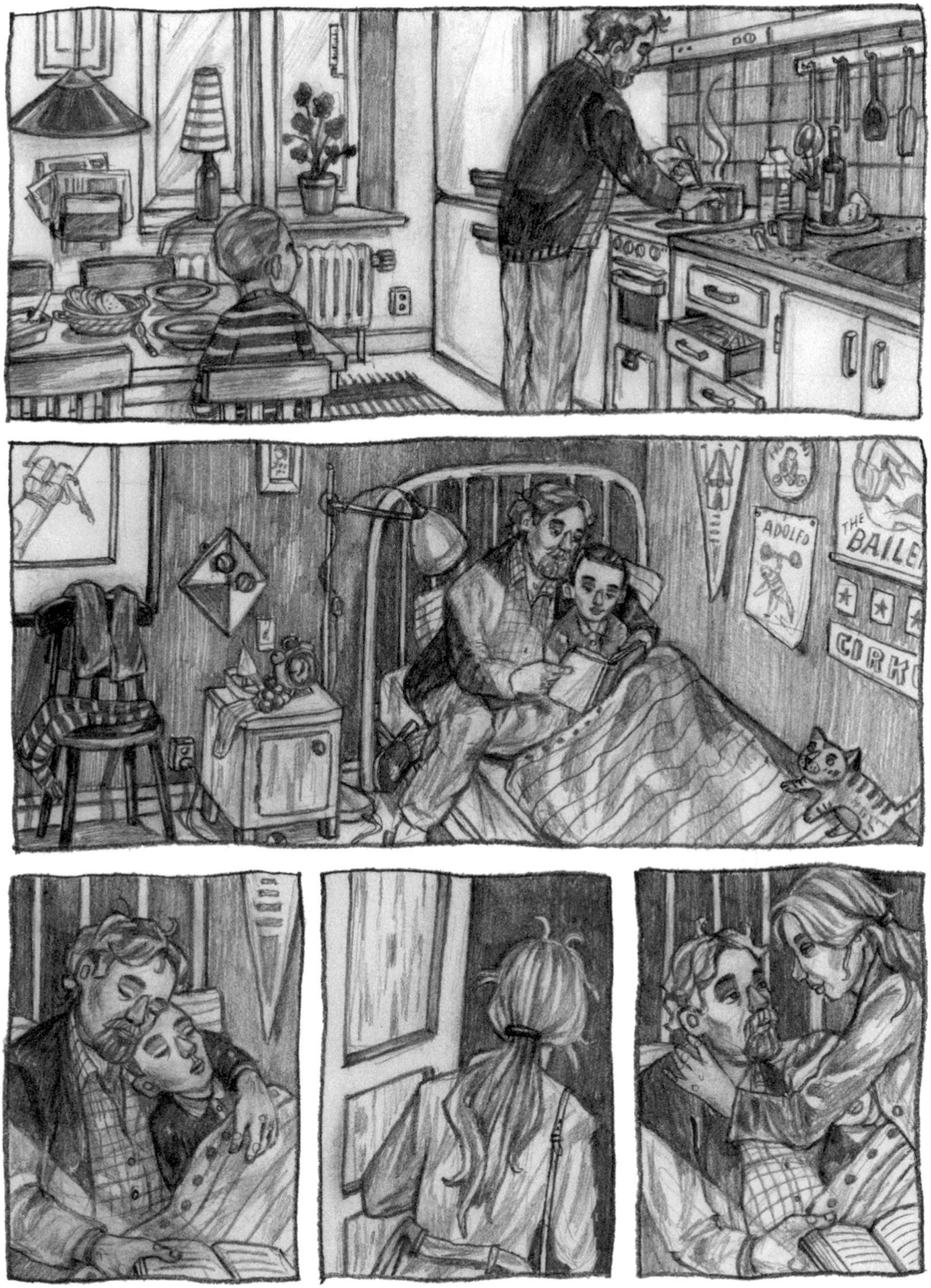
ADOLFO
THE
BAILE
CIRK

Dad worked early in the day.

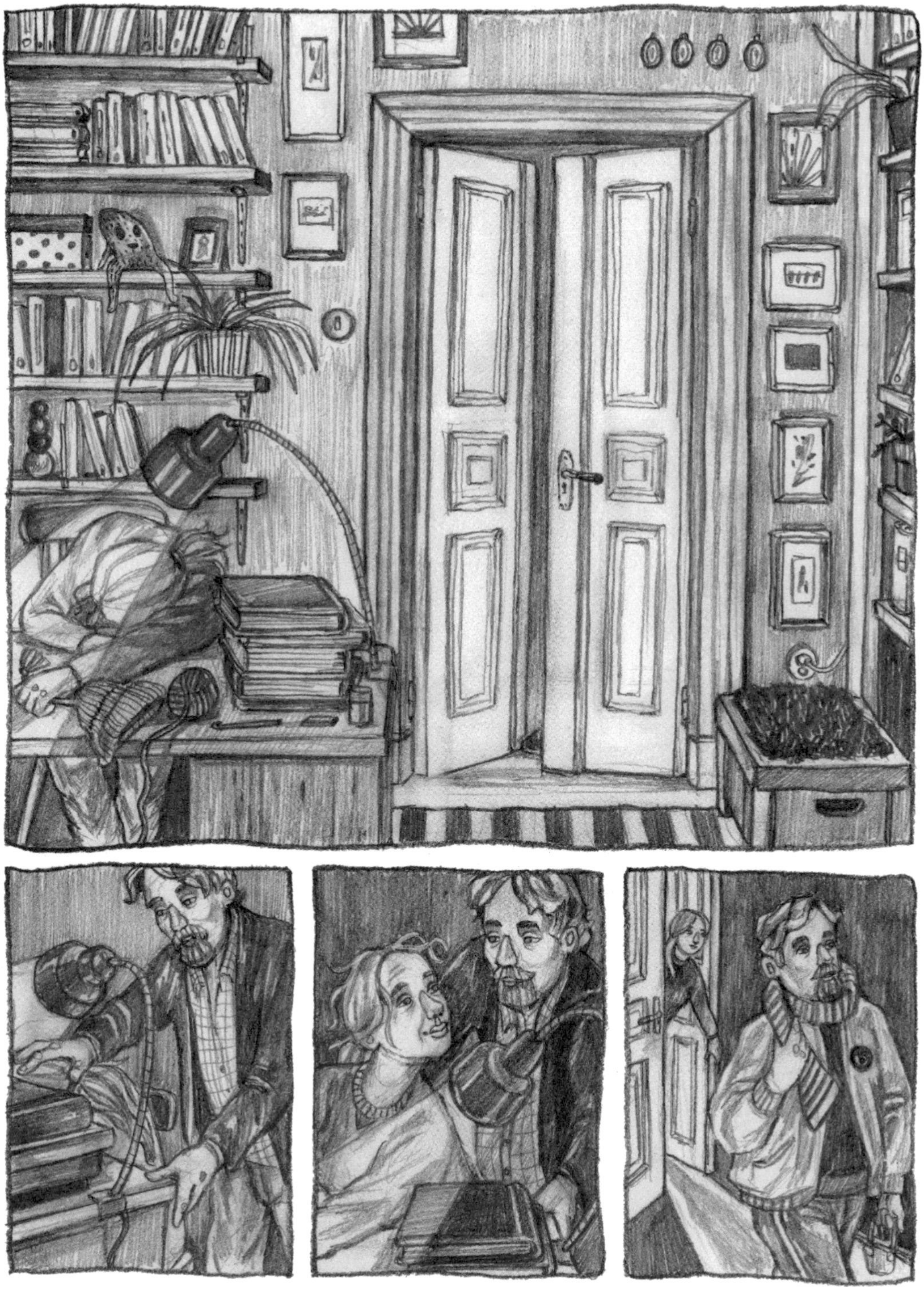

Mom worked late.

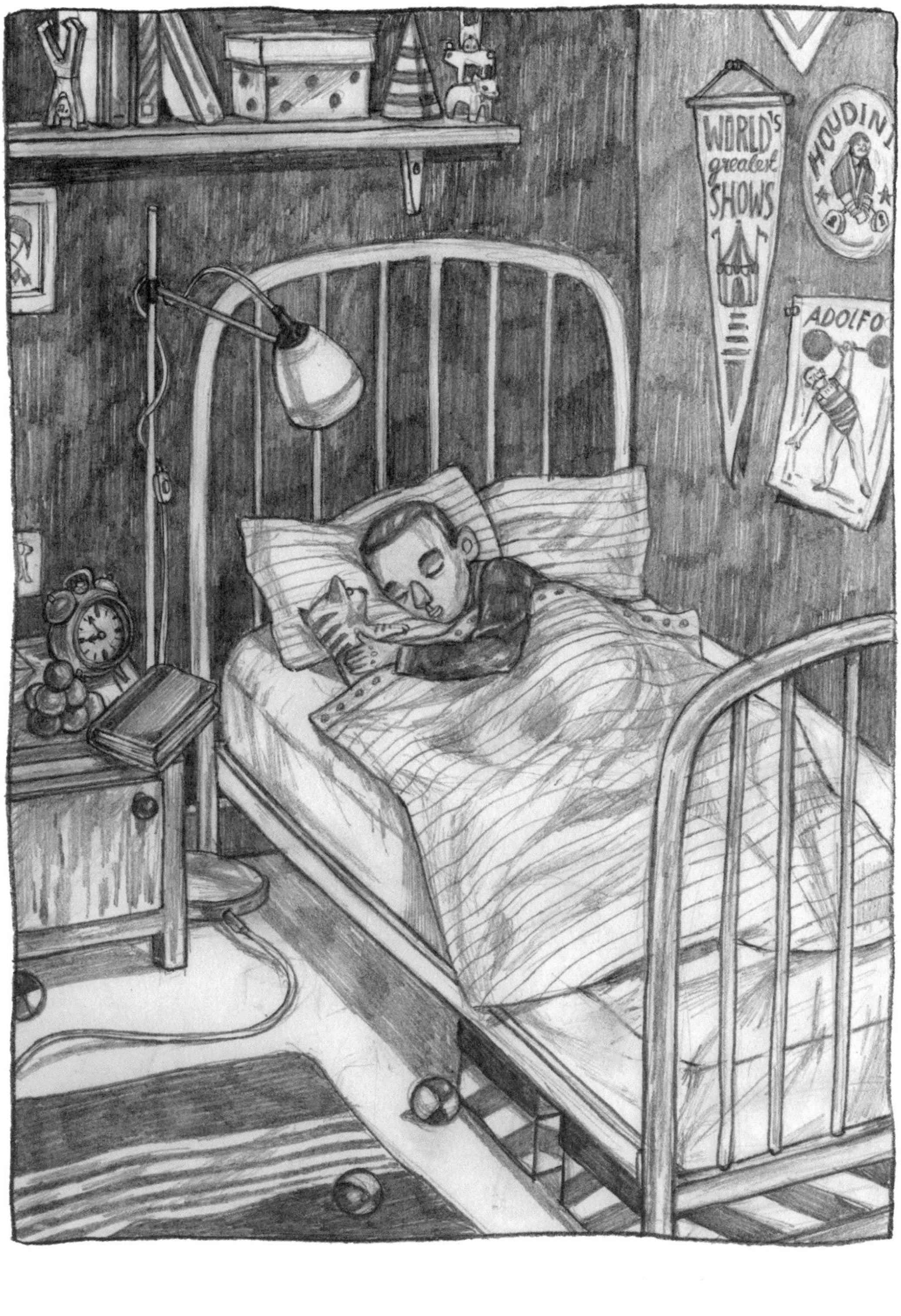
WORLD'S
greatest
SHOWS
HOUDINI
ADOLFO

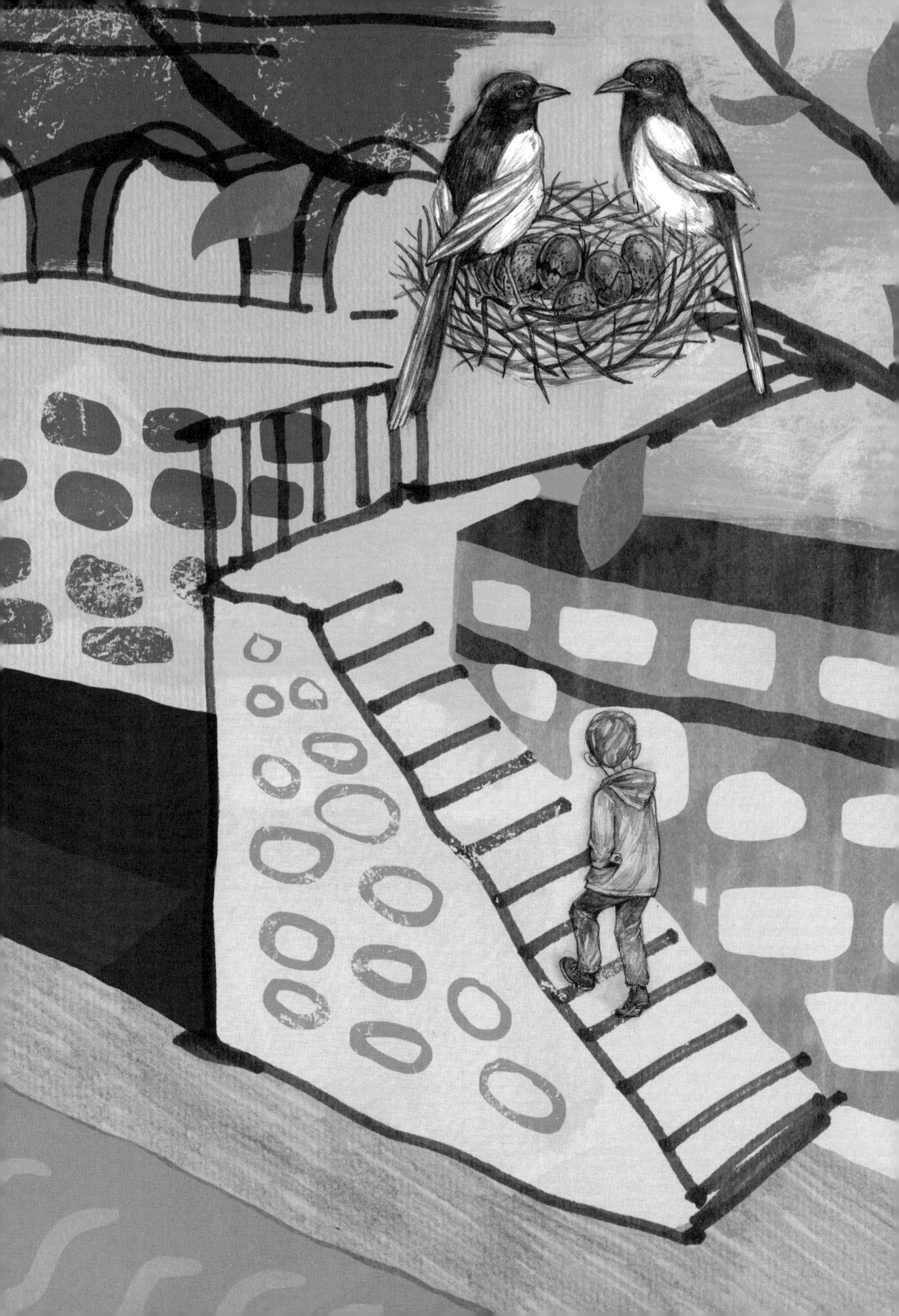

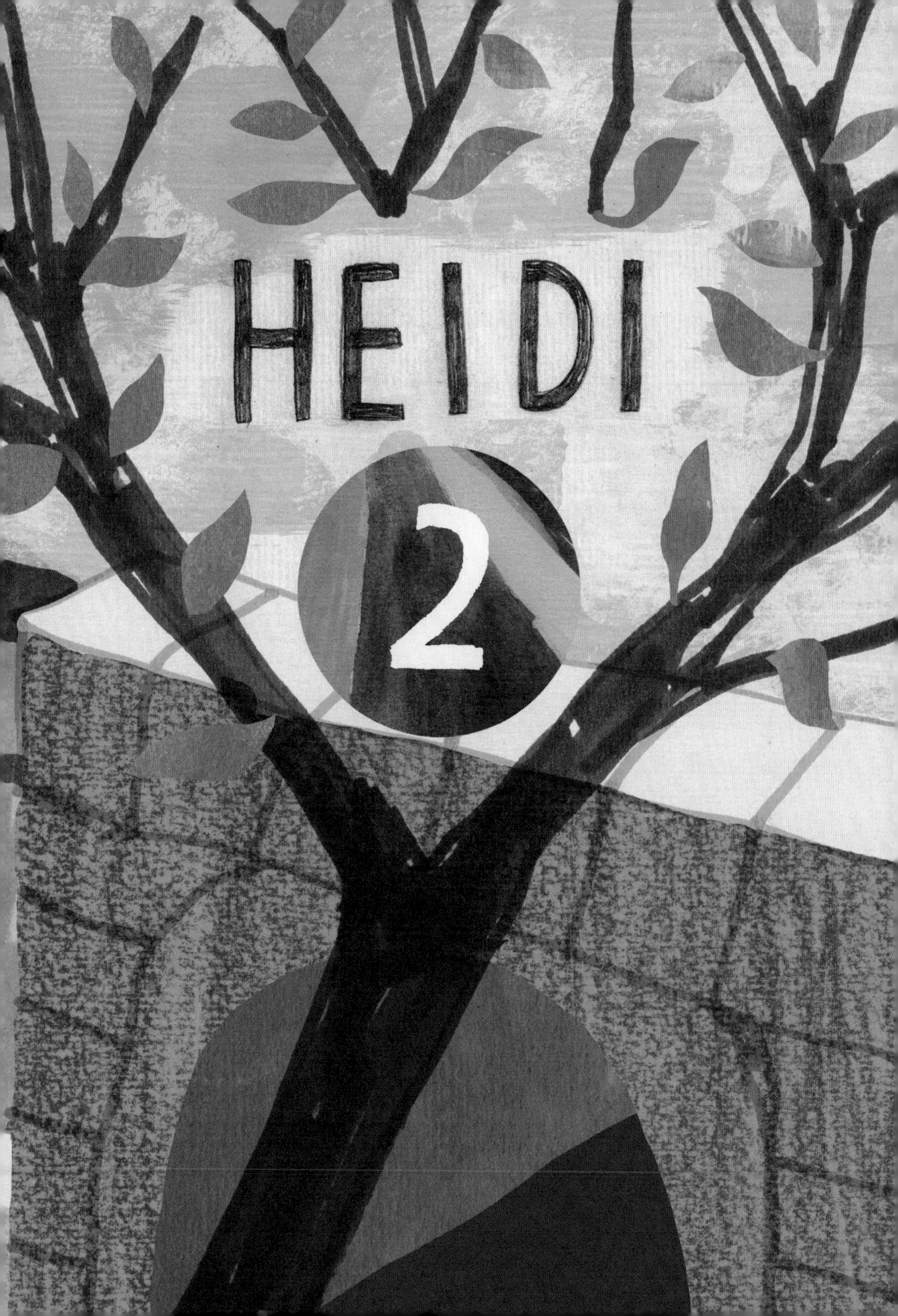
HEIDI
2

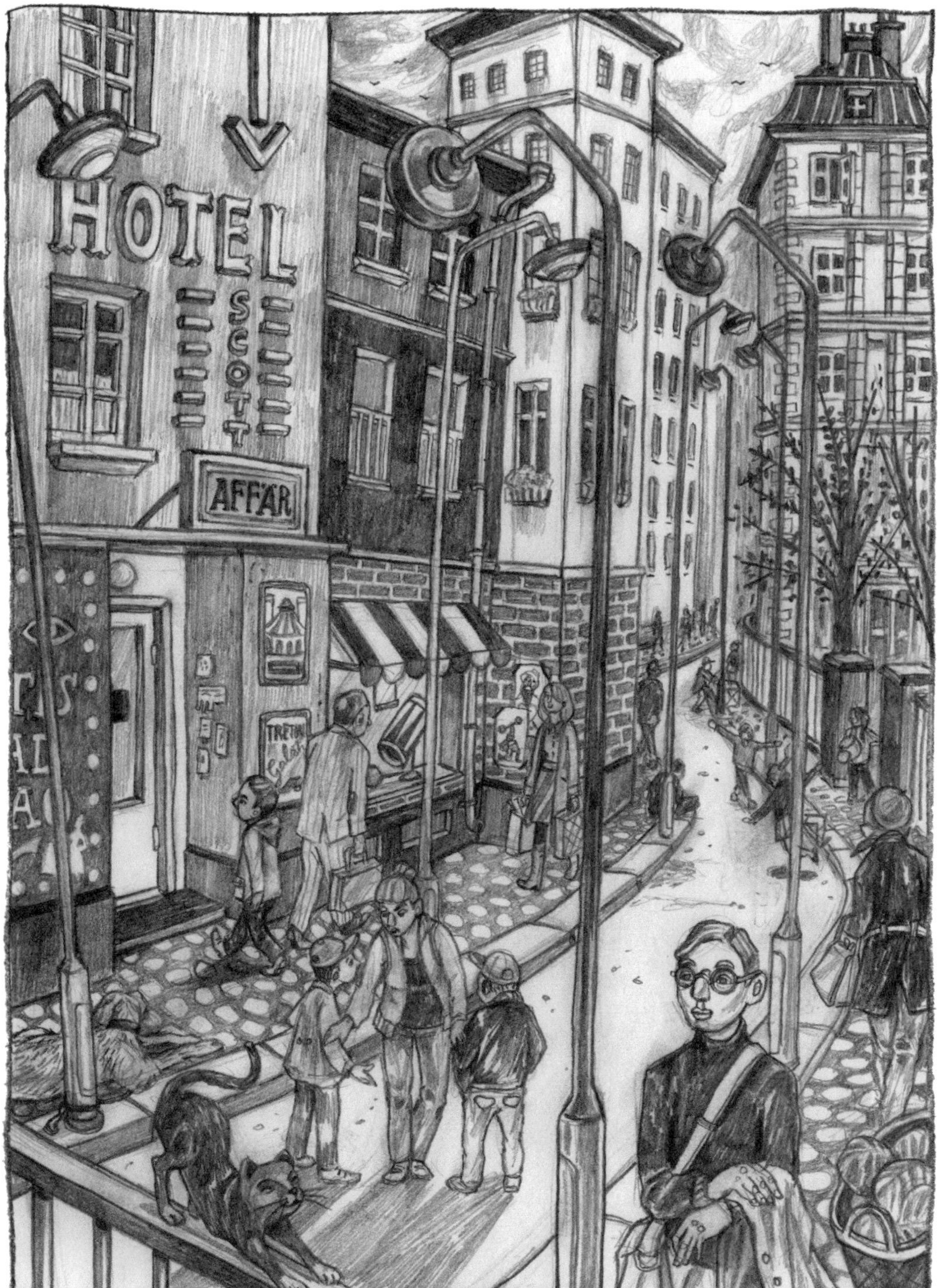
HOTEL
SCOTT
AFFÄR

I met Heidi totally by chance.

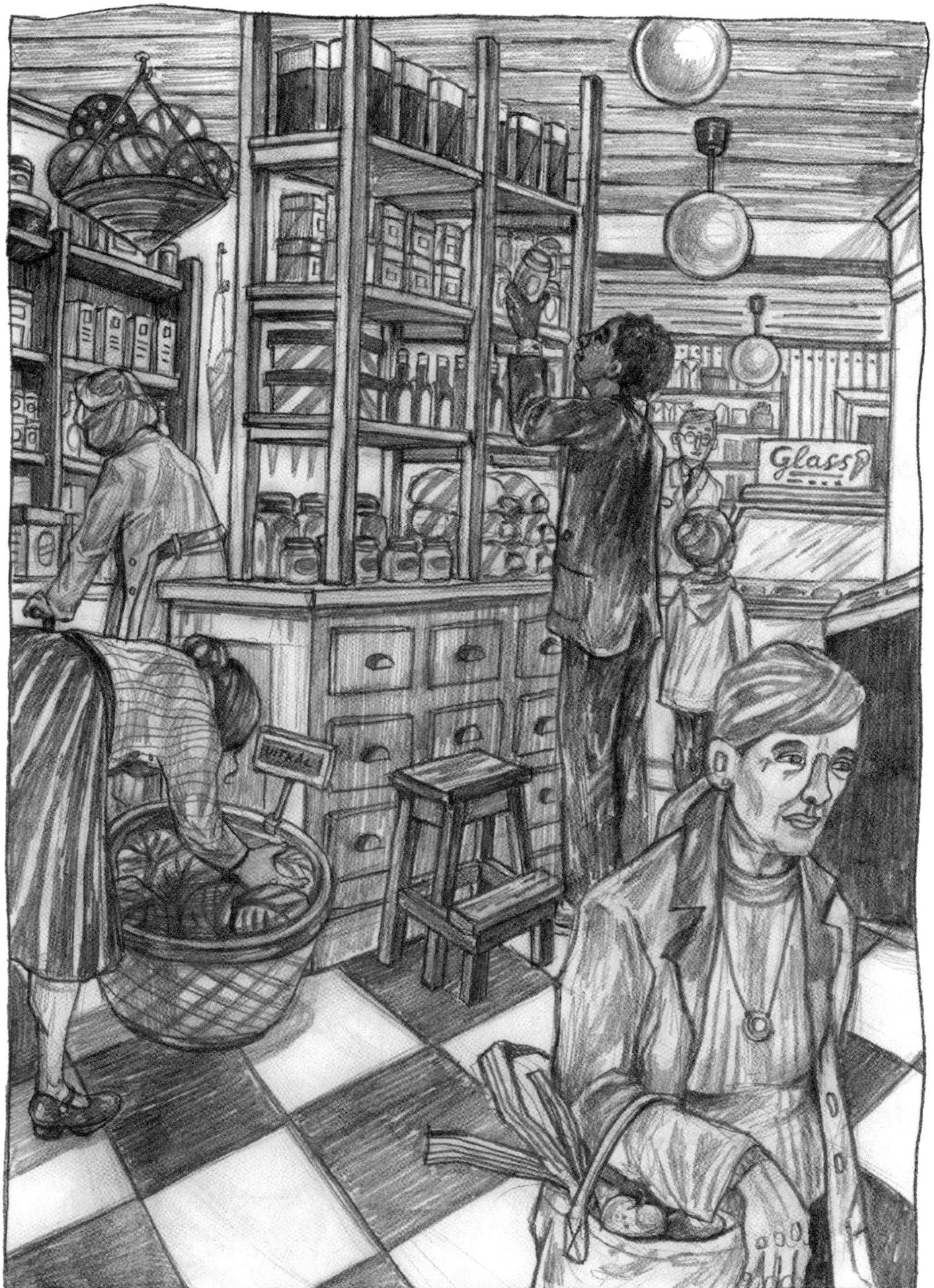
Glass
VITKÅL

I had gone to the store to get ice cream.

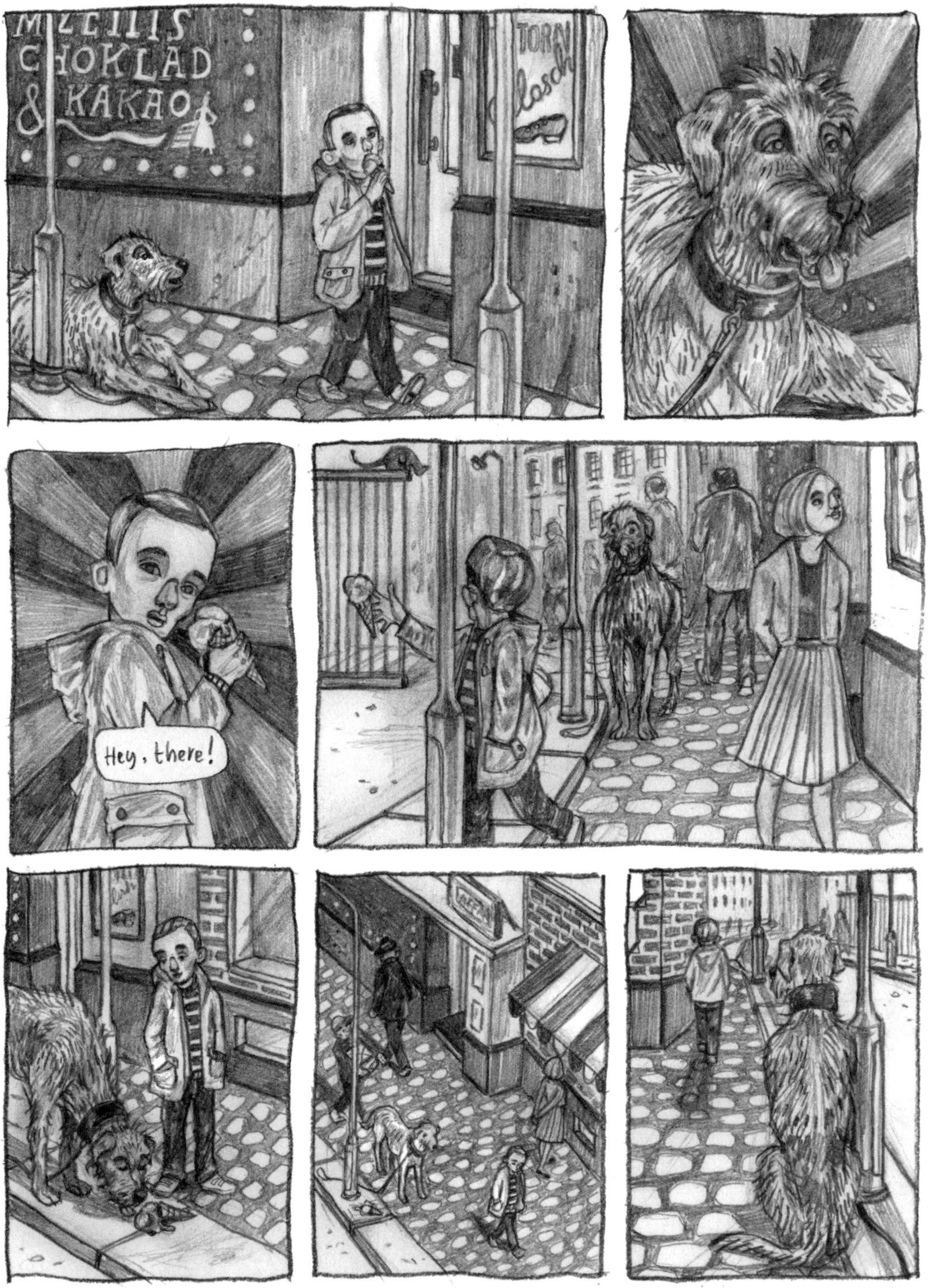
CHOKLAD
& KAKAO
Hey, there!

She was waiting for me outside. We shared the ice cream.

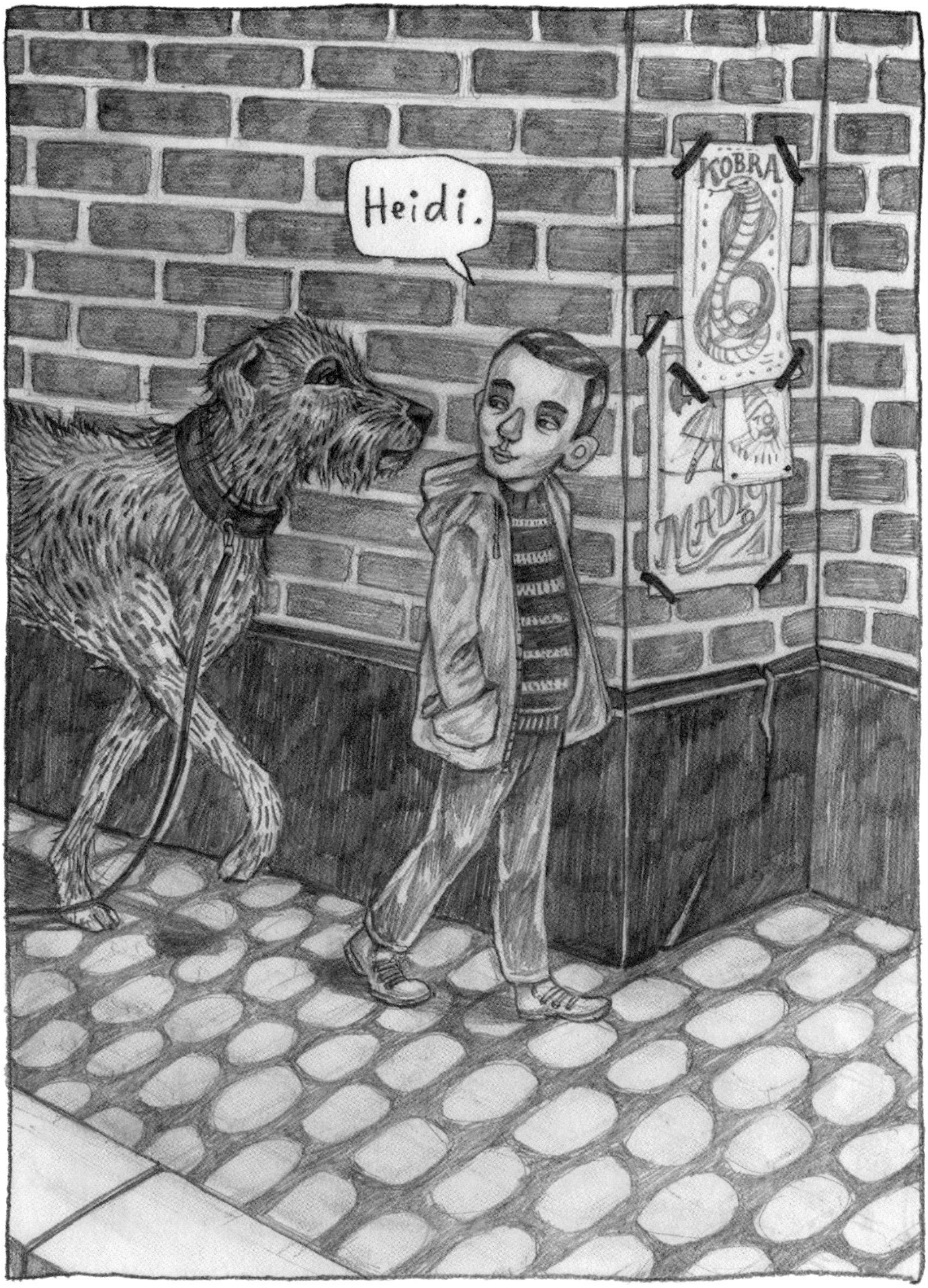
Heidi.
KOBRA

Then she followed me home.

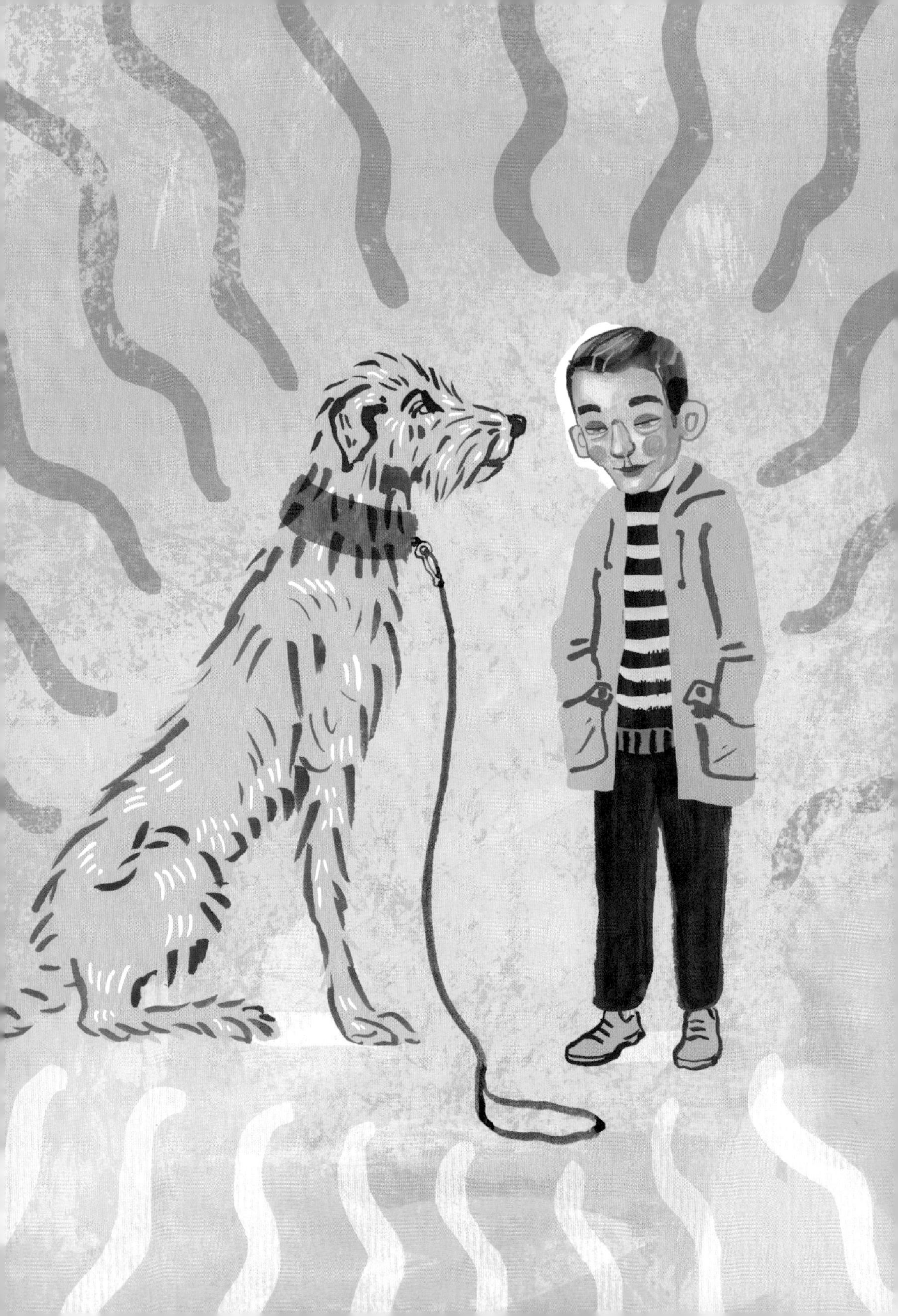

At first, it felt a little strange.

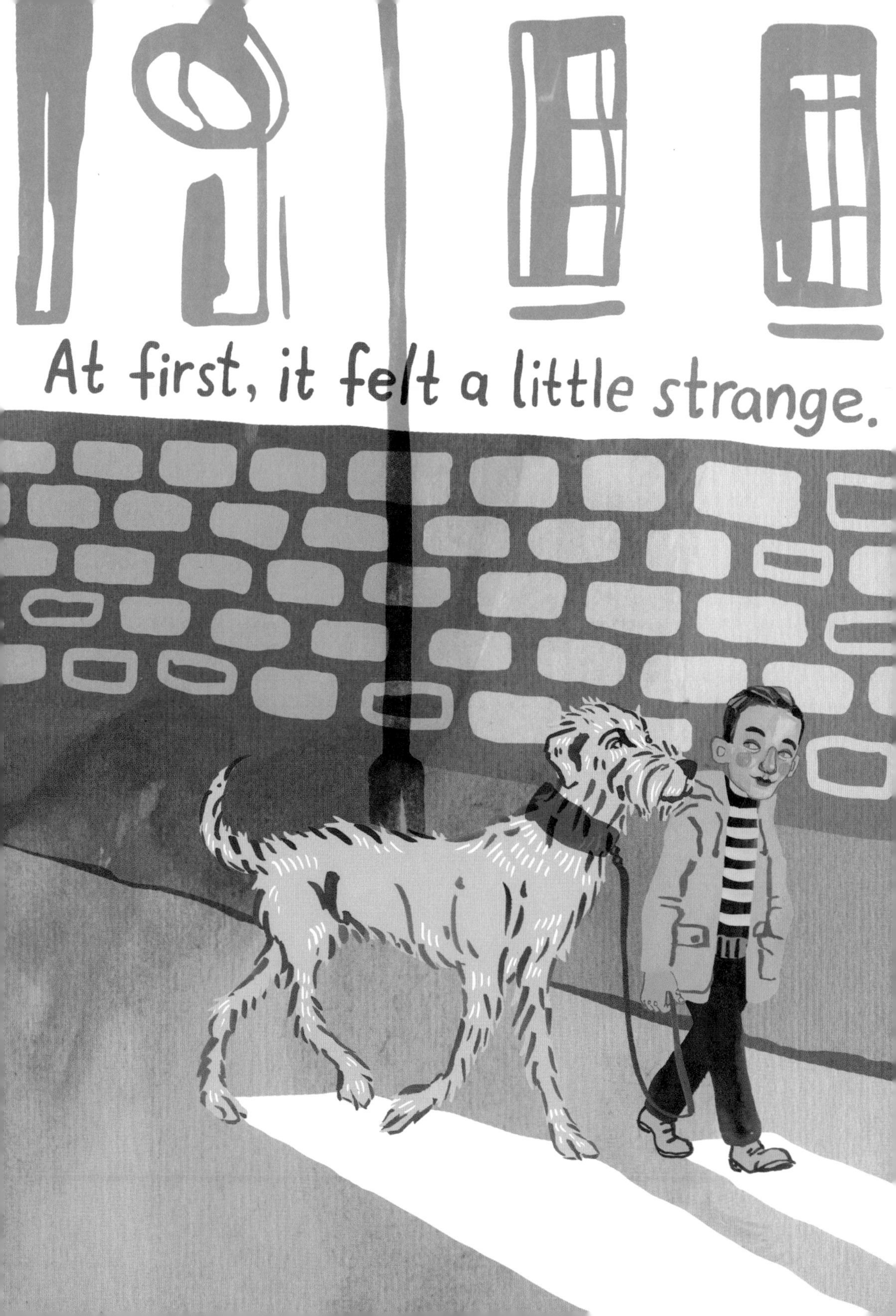

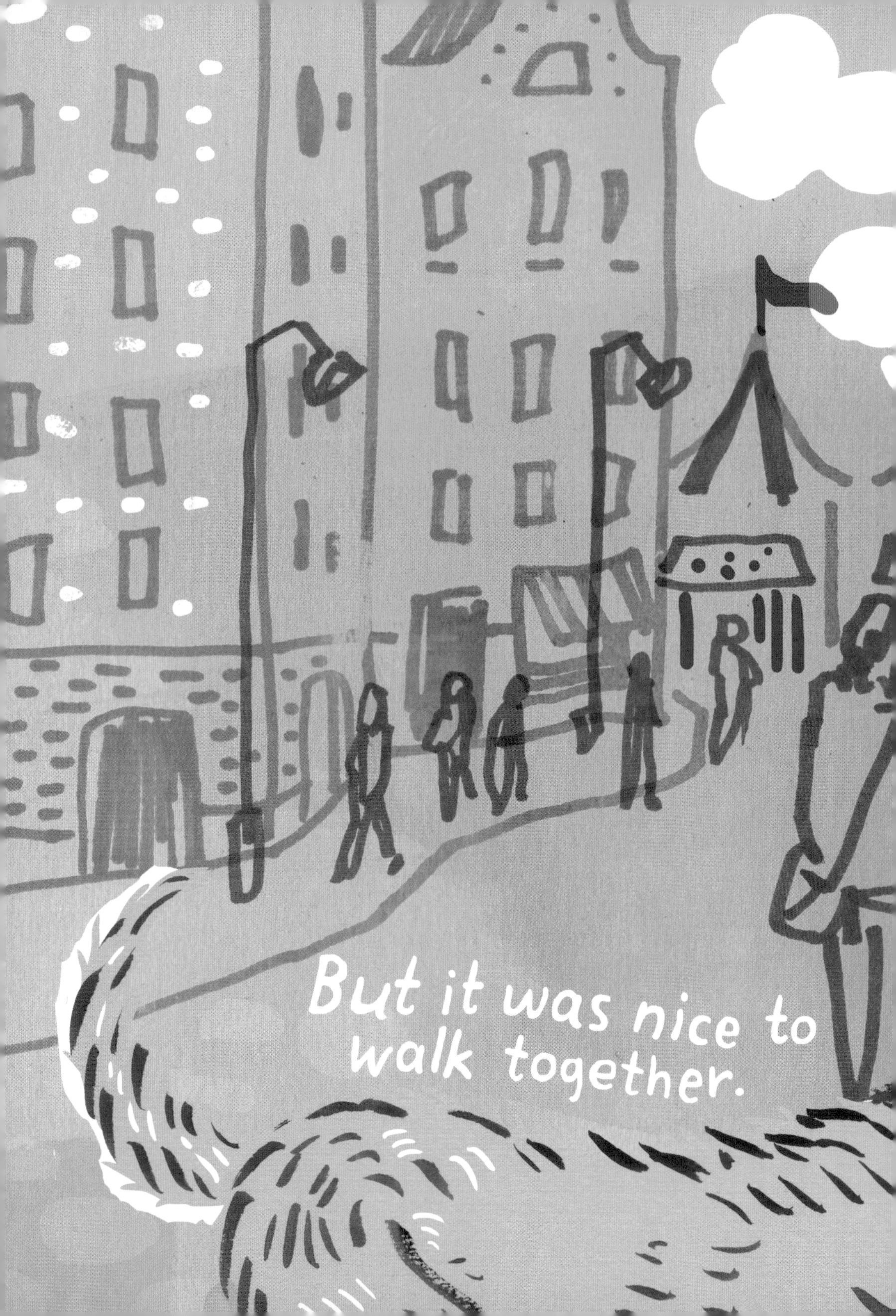

But it was nice to
walk together.

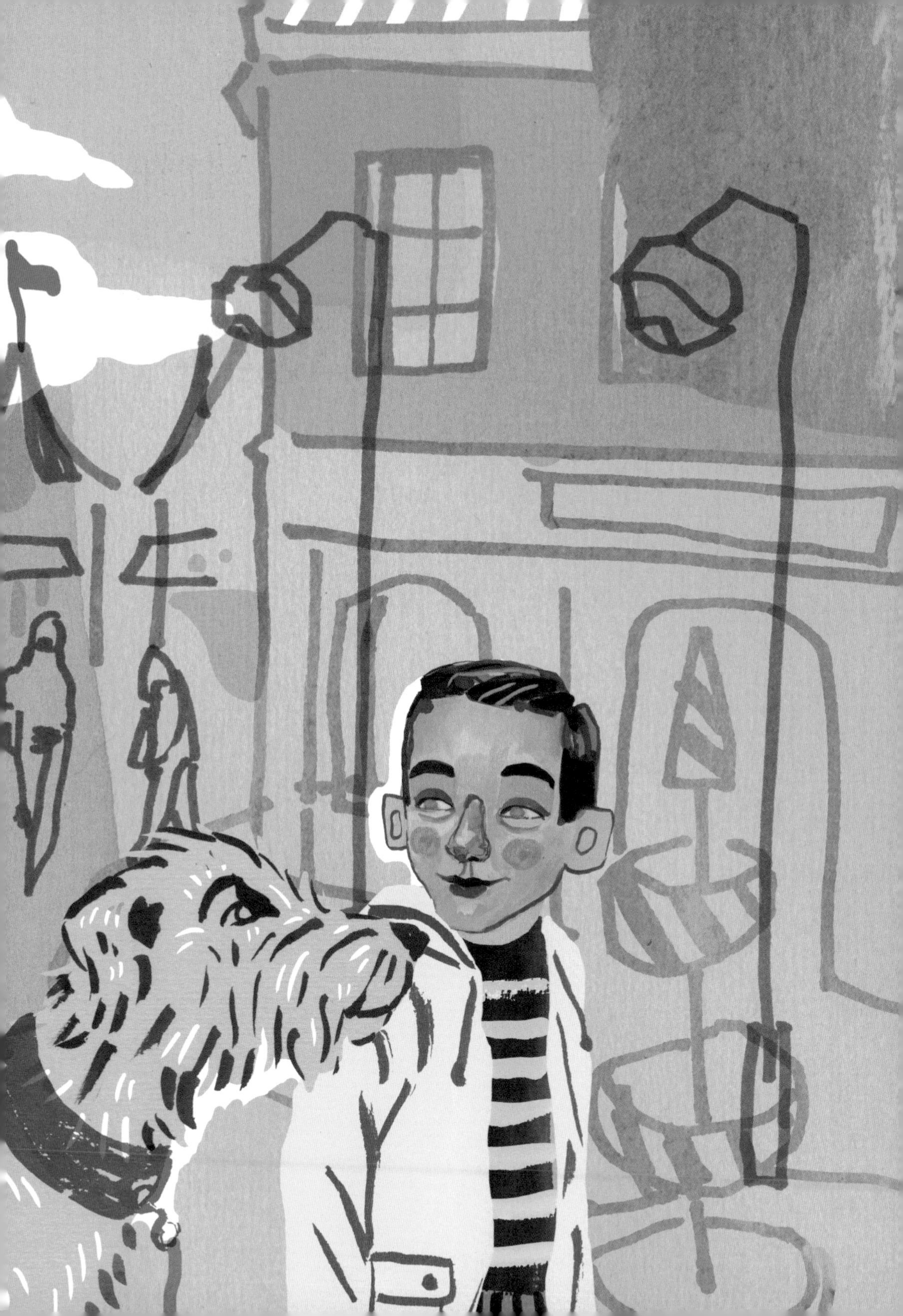

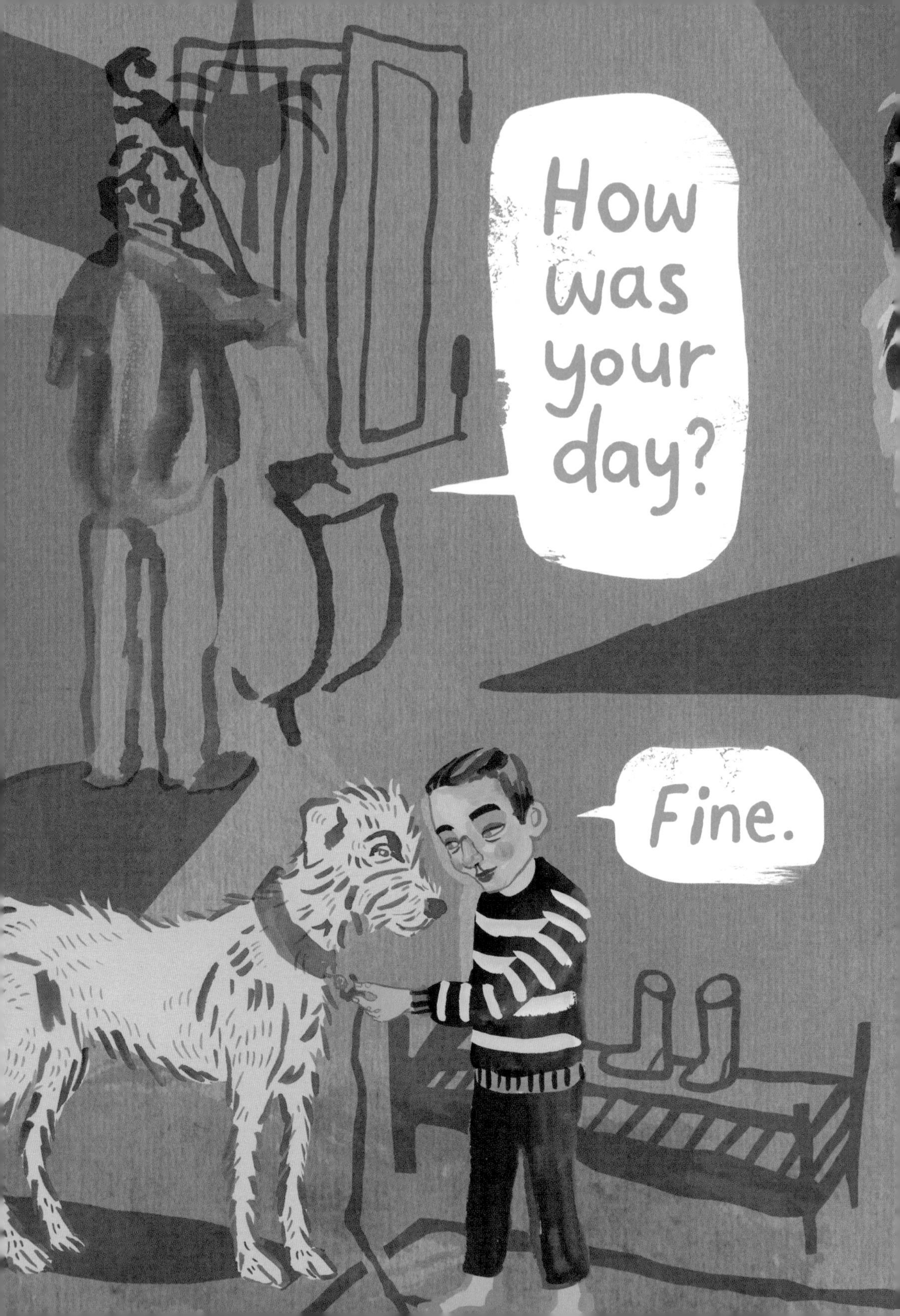
How was your day?
Fine.

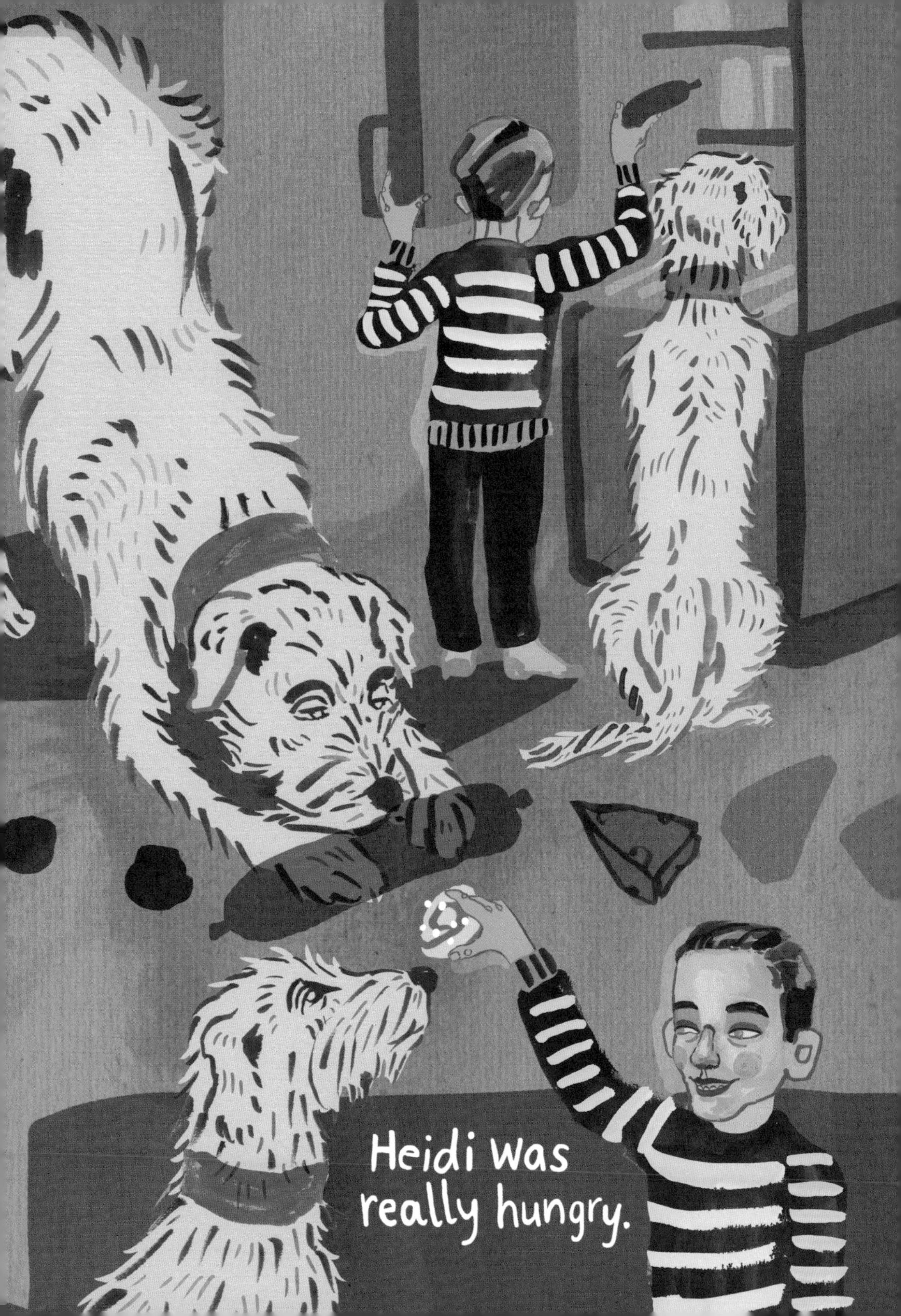

Heidi was really hungry.

Then she got tired.

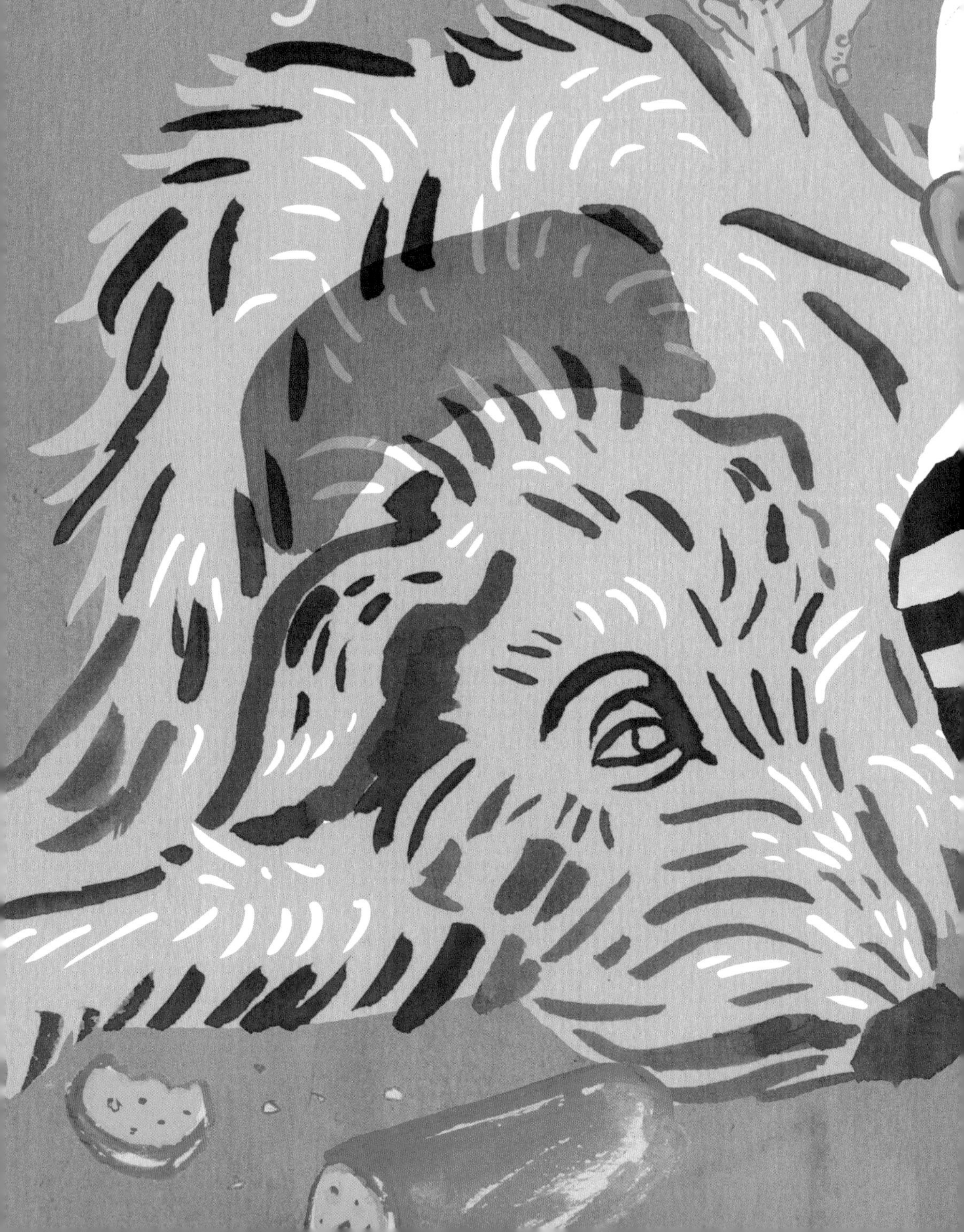

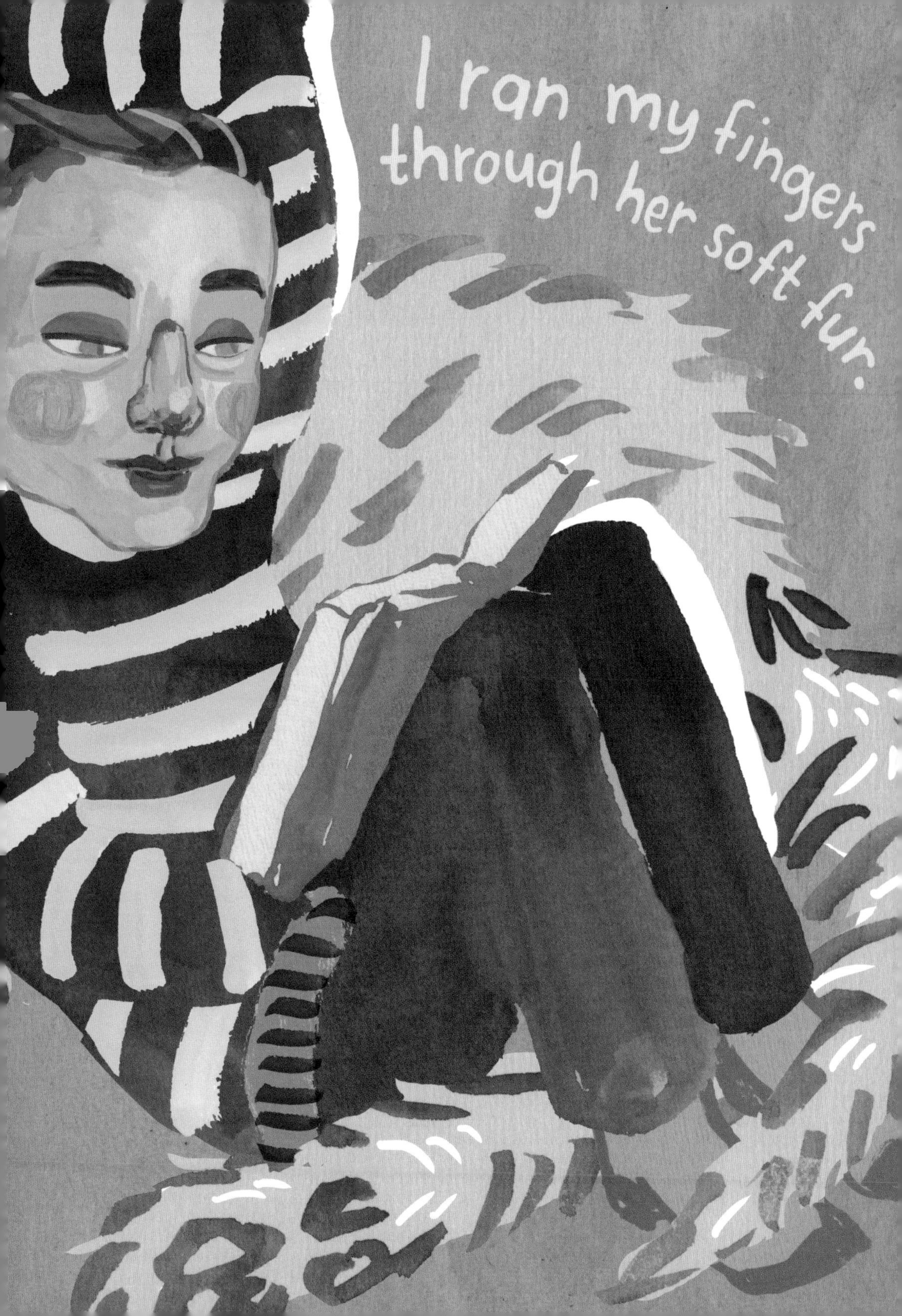
I ran my fingers through her soft fur.

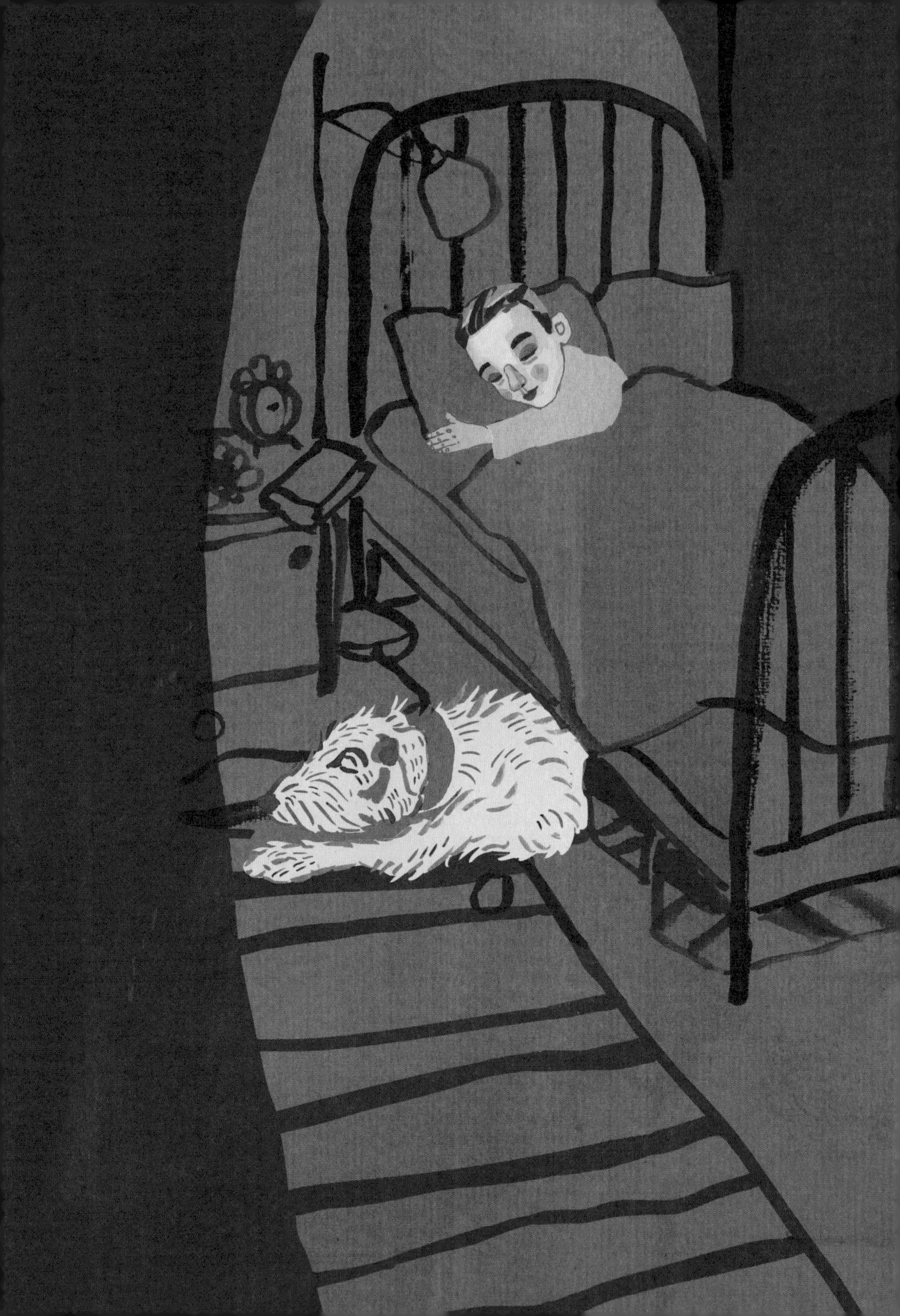

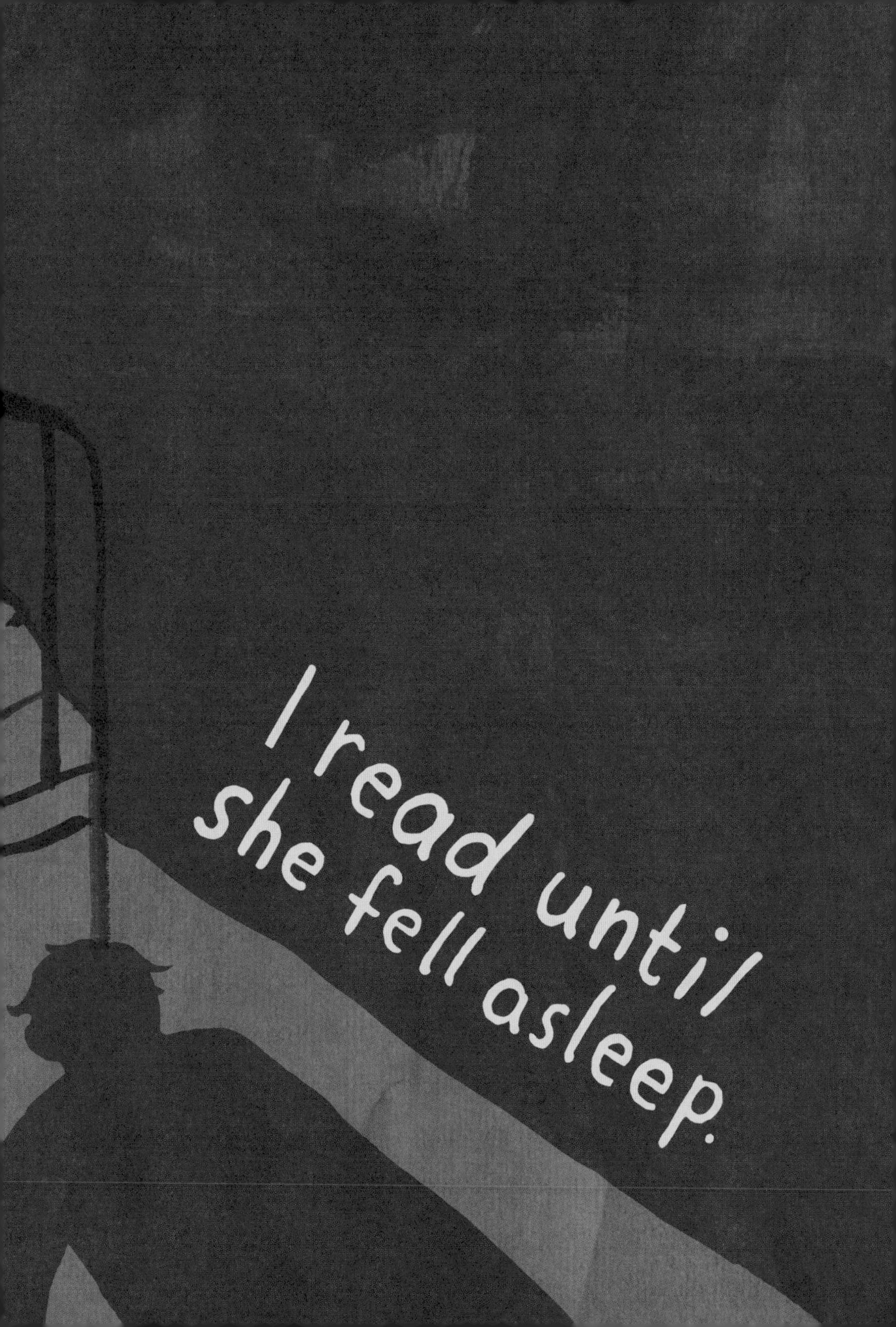
I read until
she fell asleep.

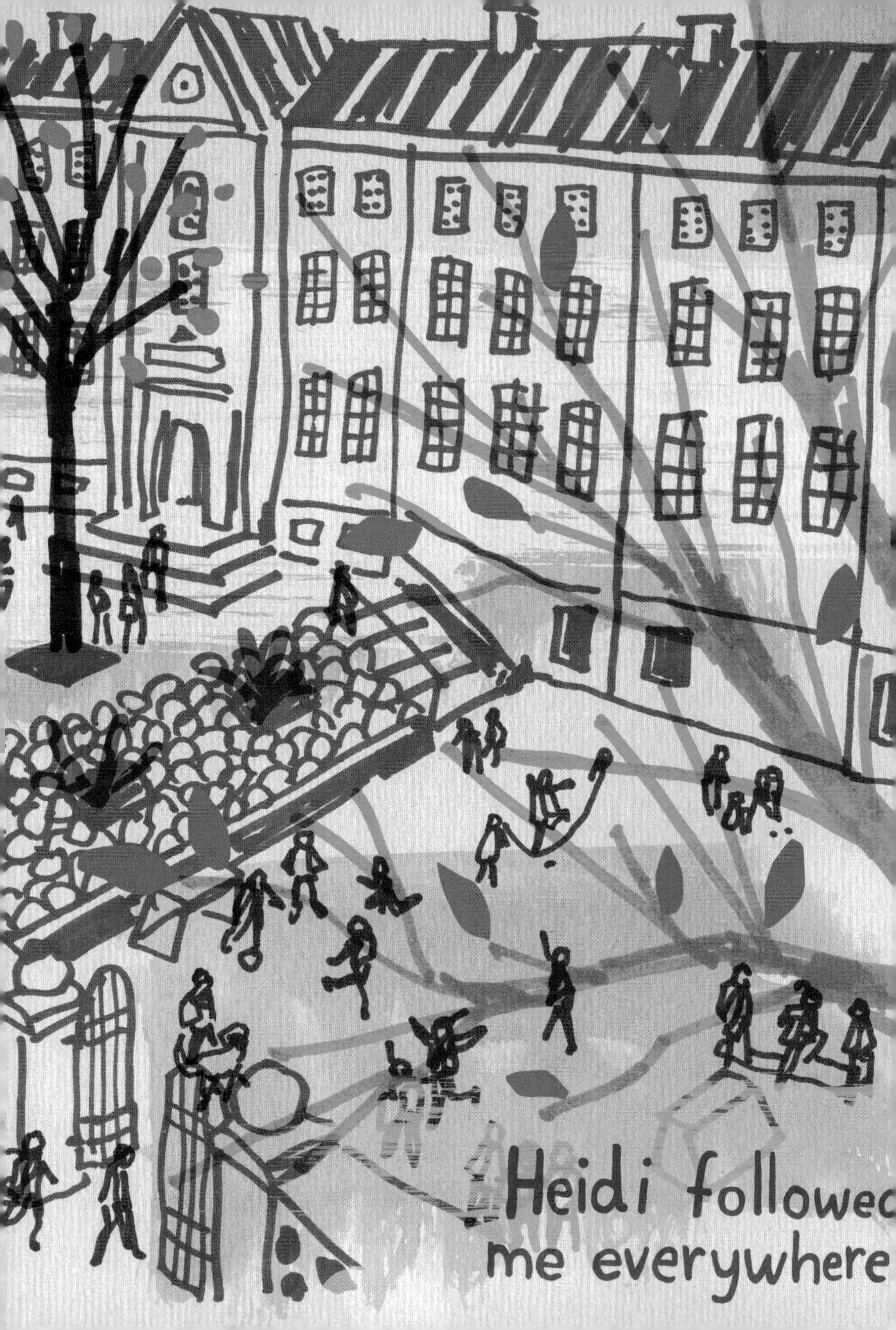

Heidi followed
me everywhere

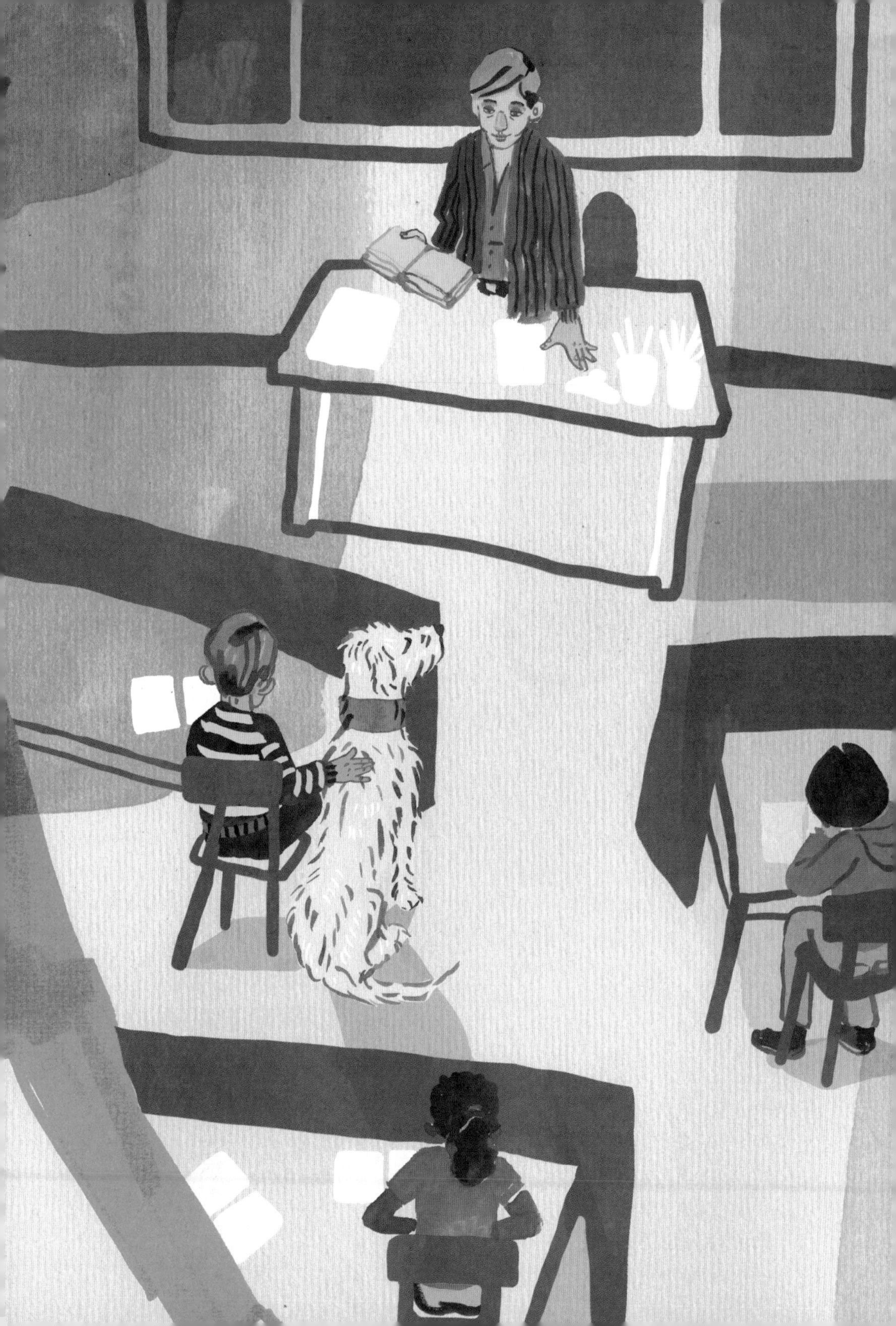

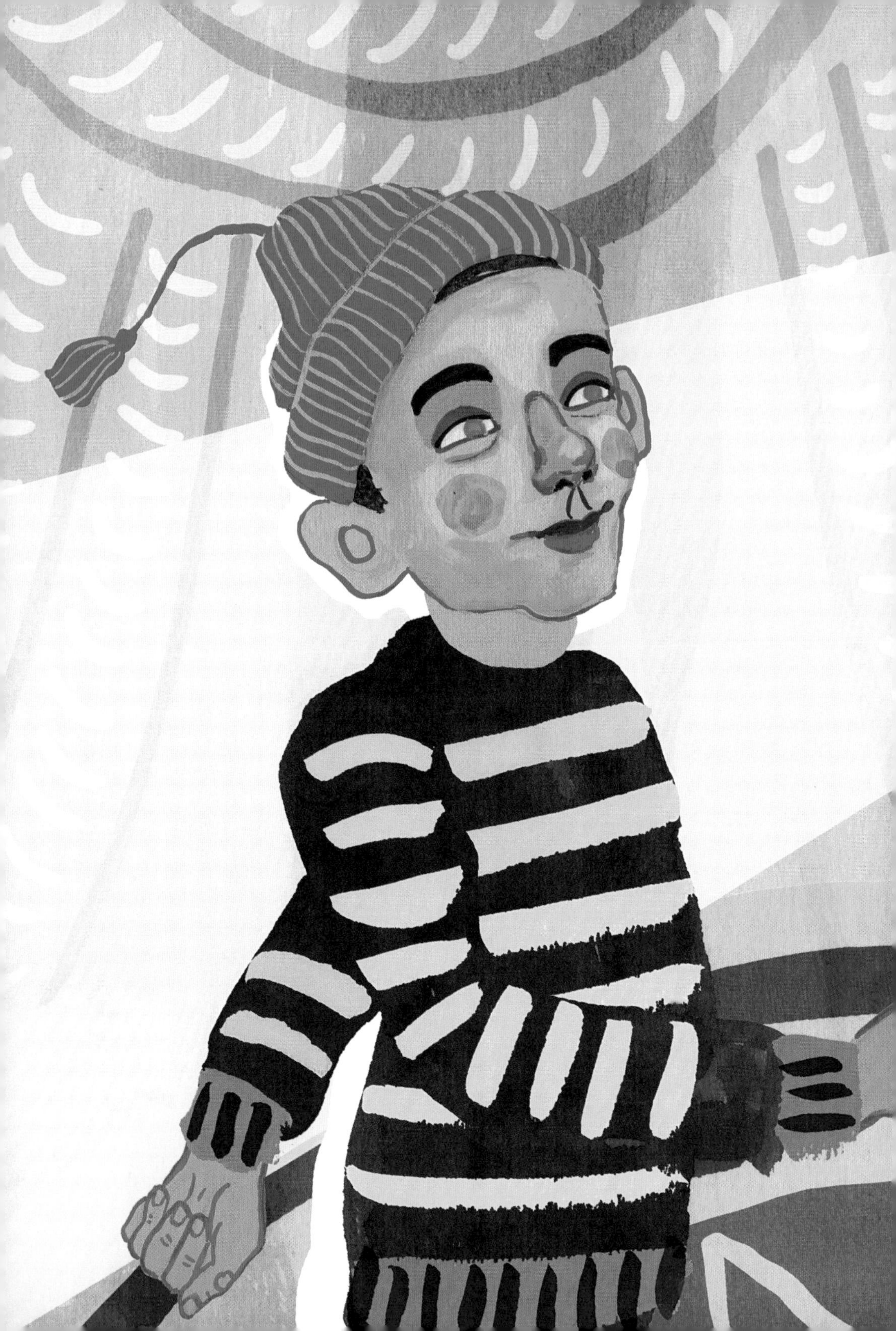

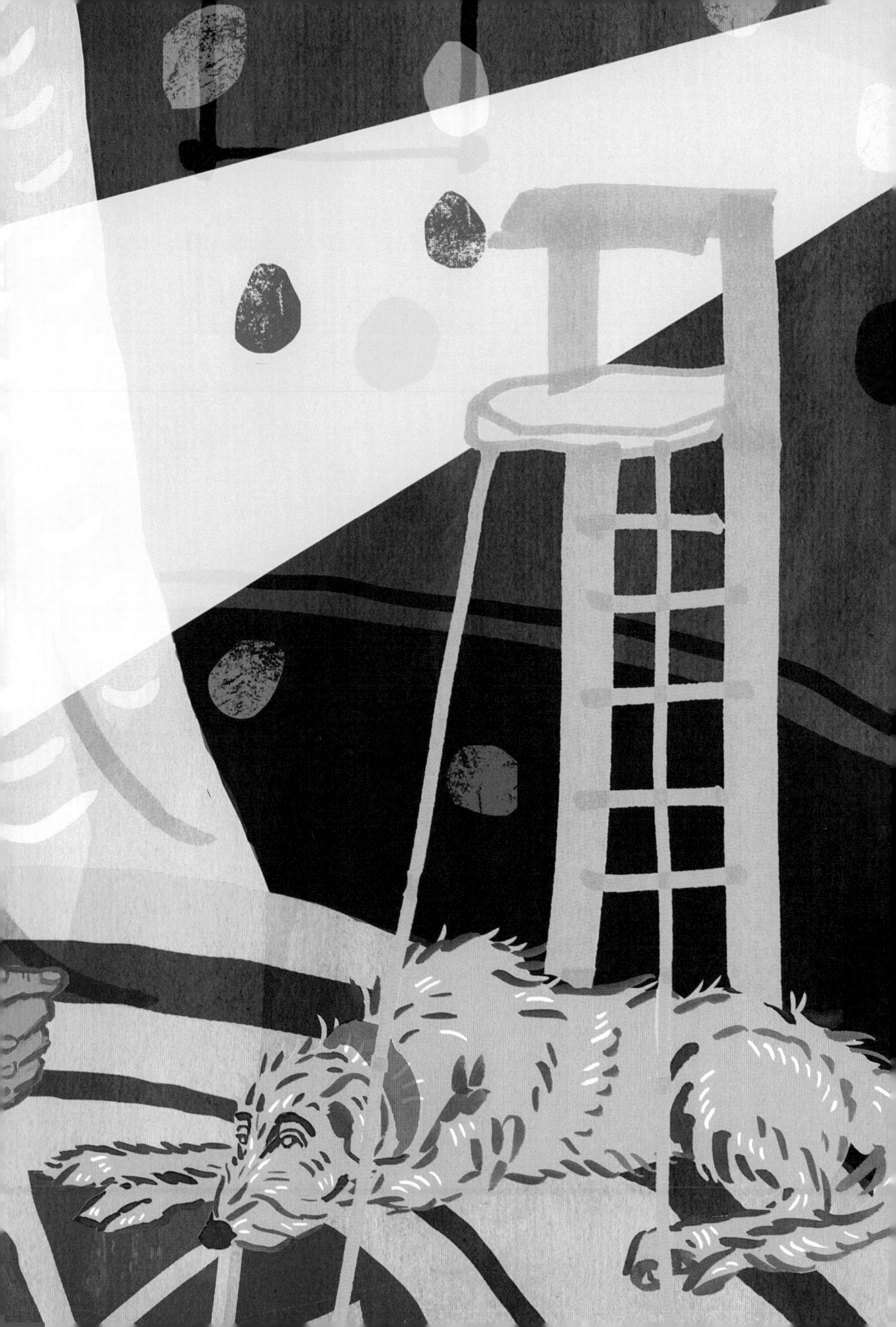

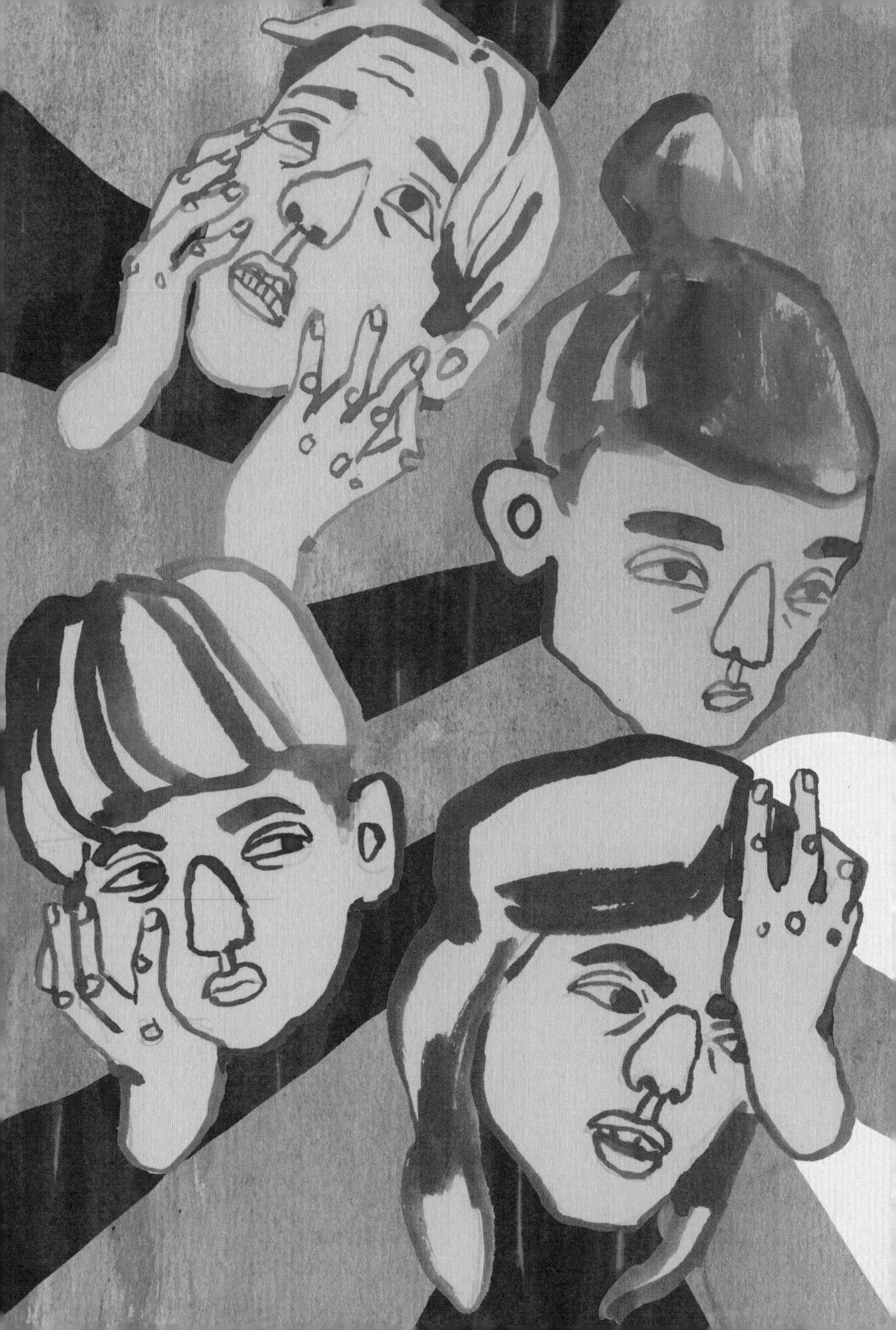

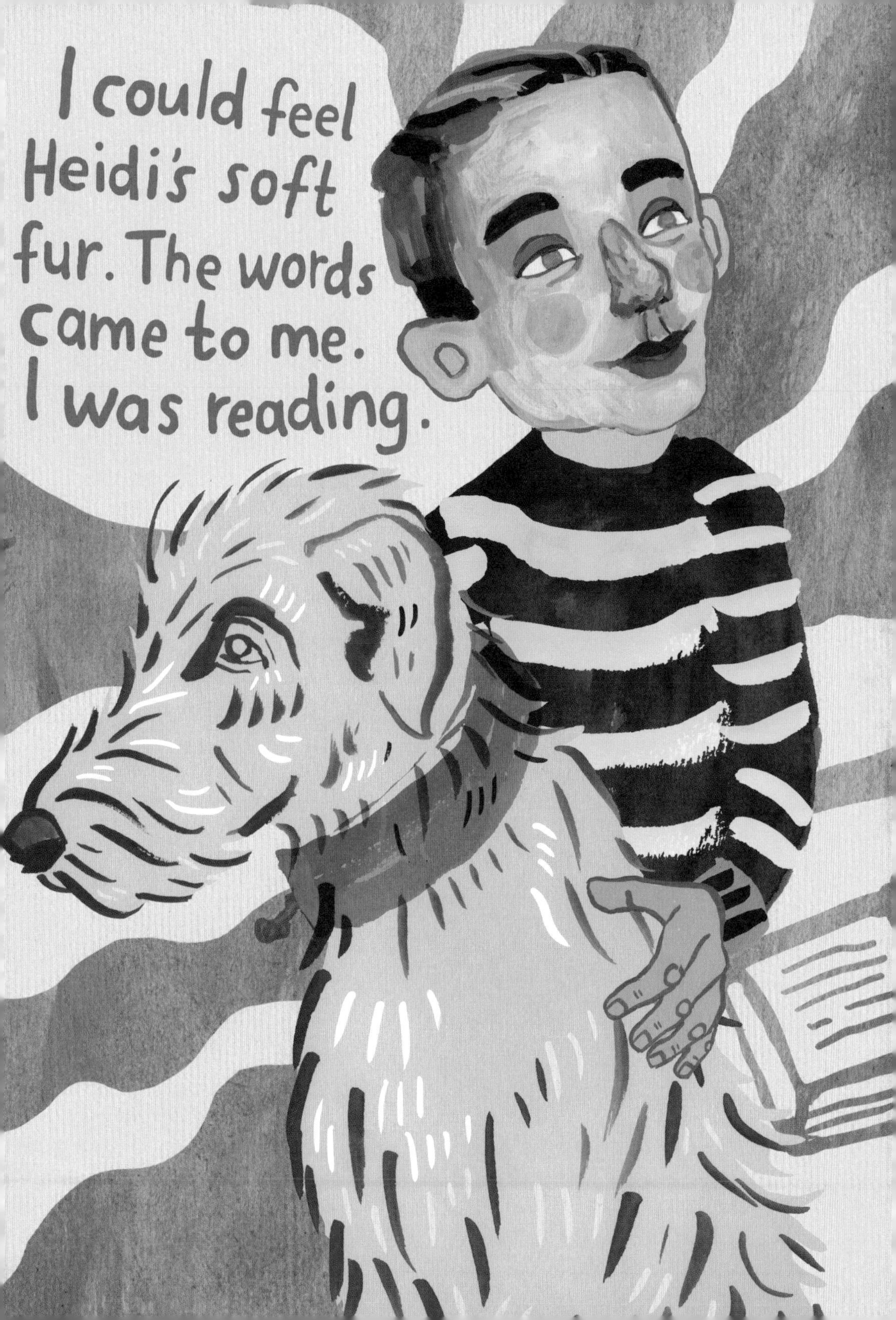
I could feel Heidi's soft fur. The words came to me. I was reading.

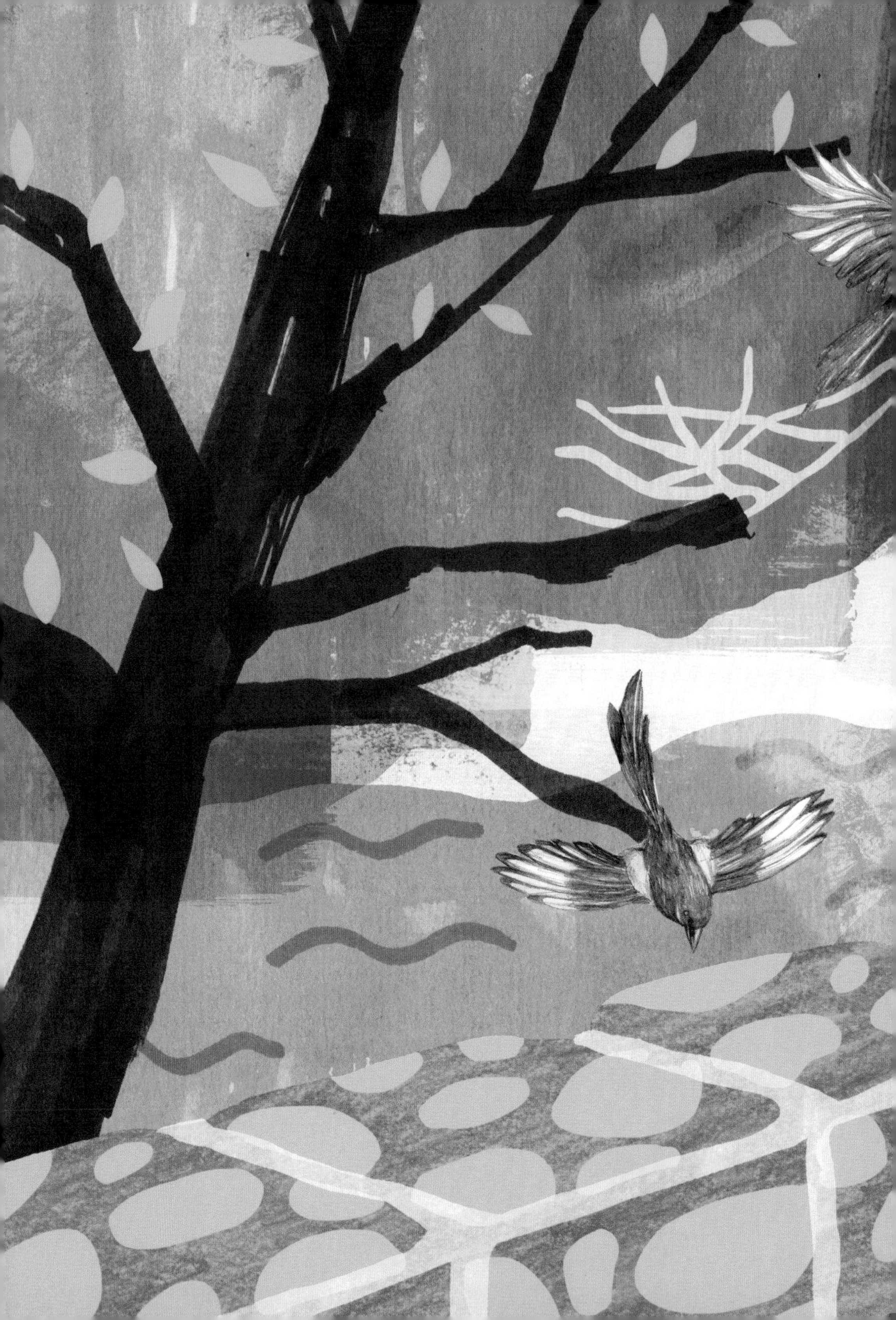

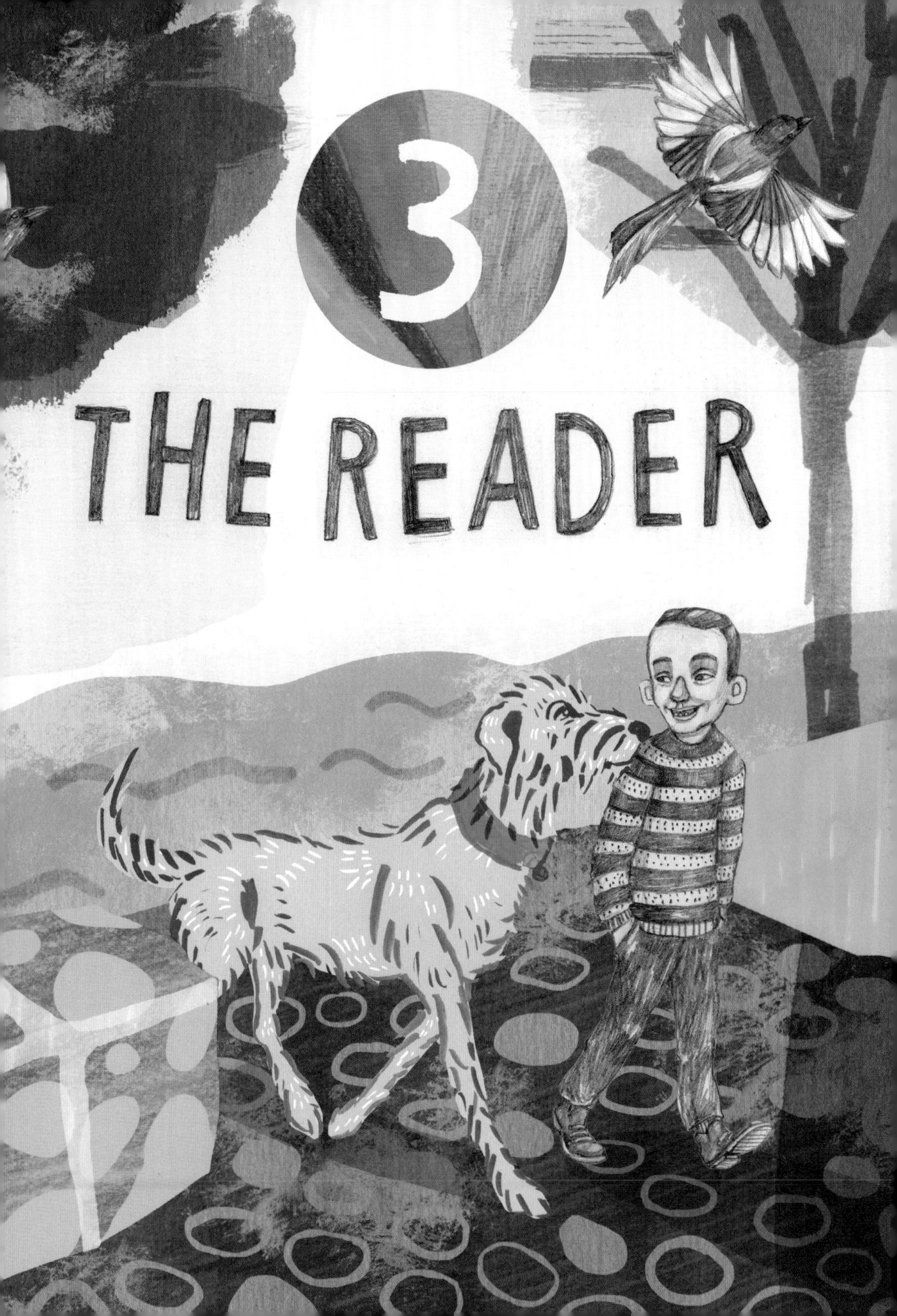
3
THE READER

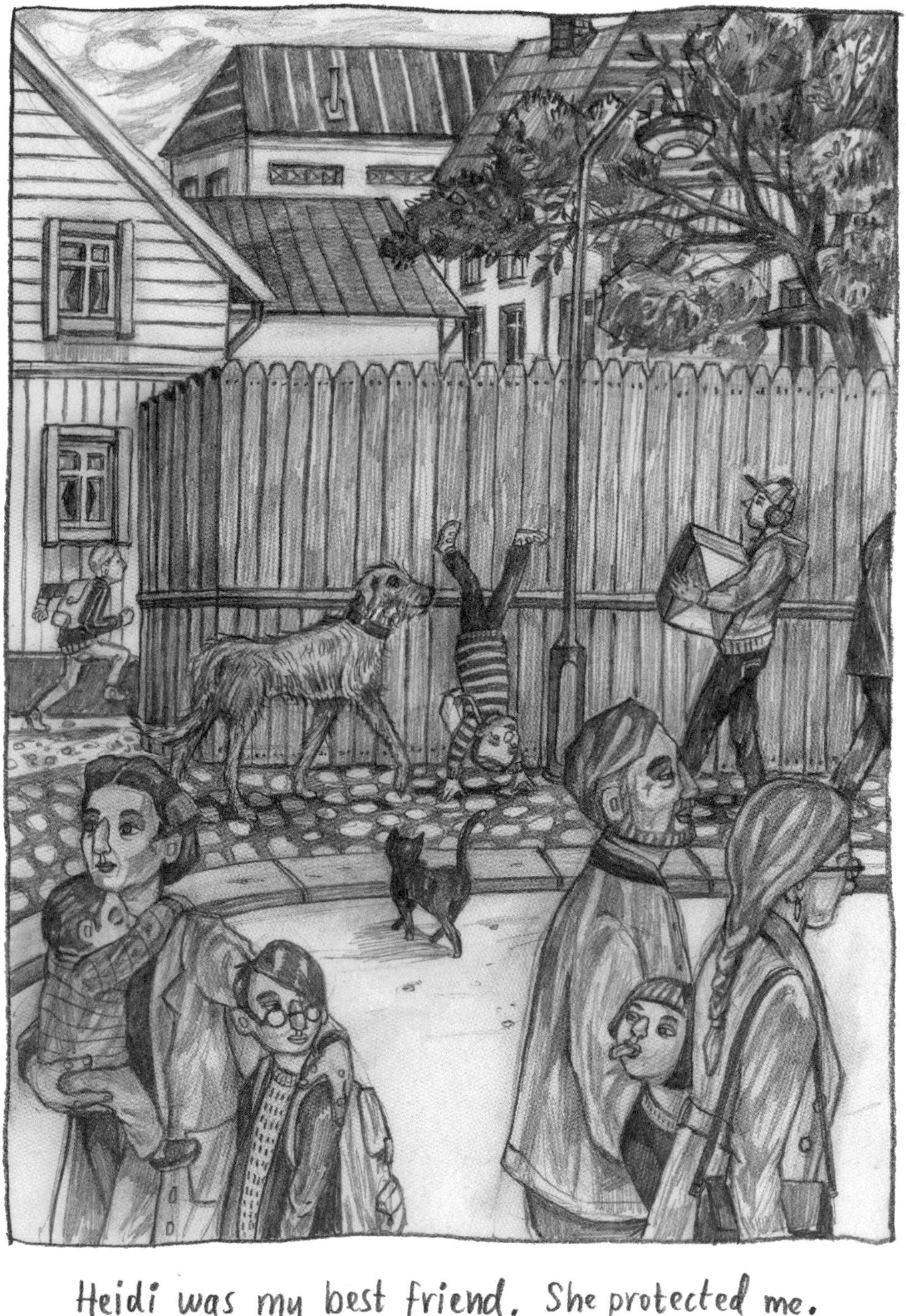

Heidi was my best friend. She protected me.

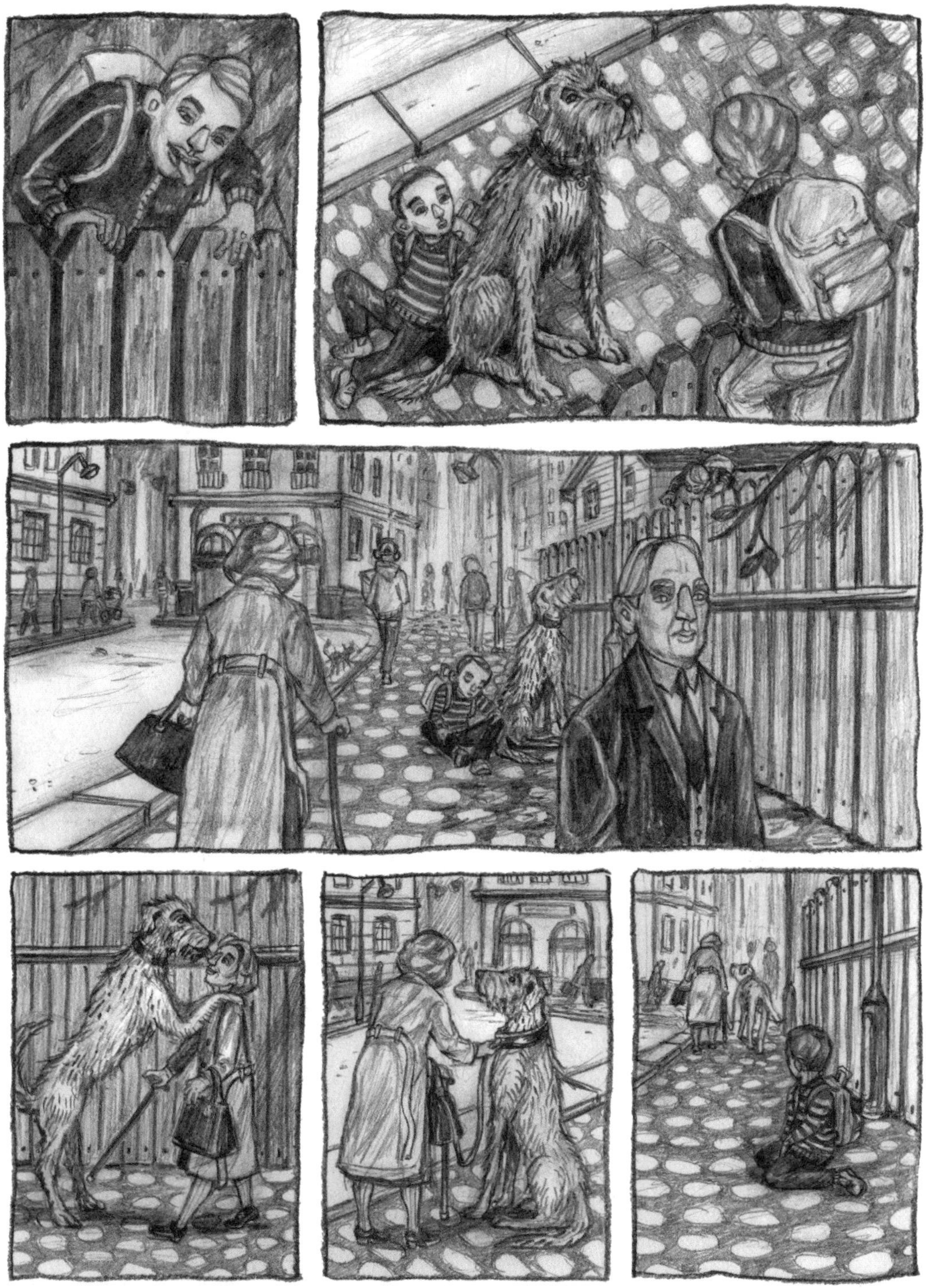

We were always together. But then something happened.

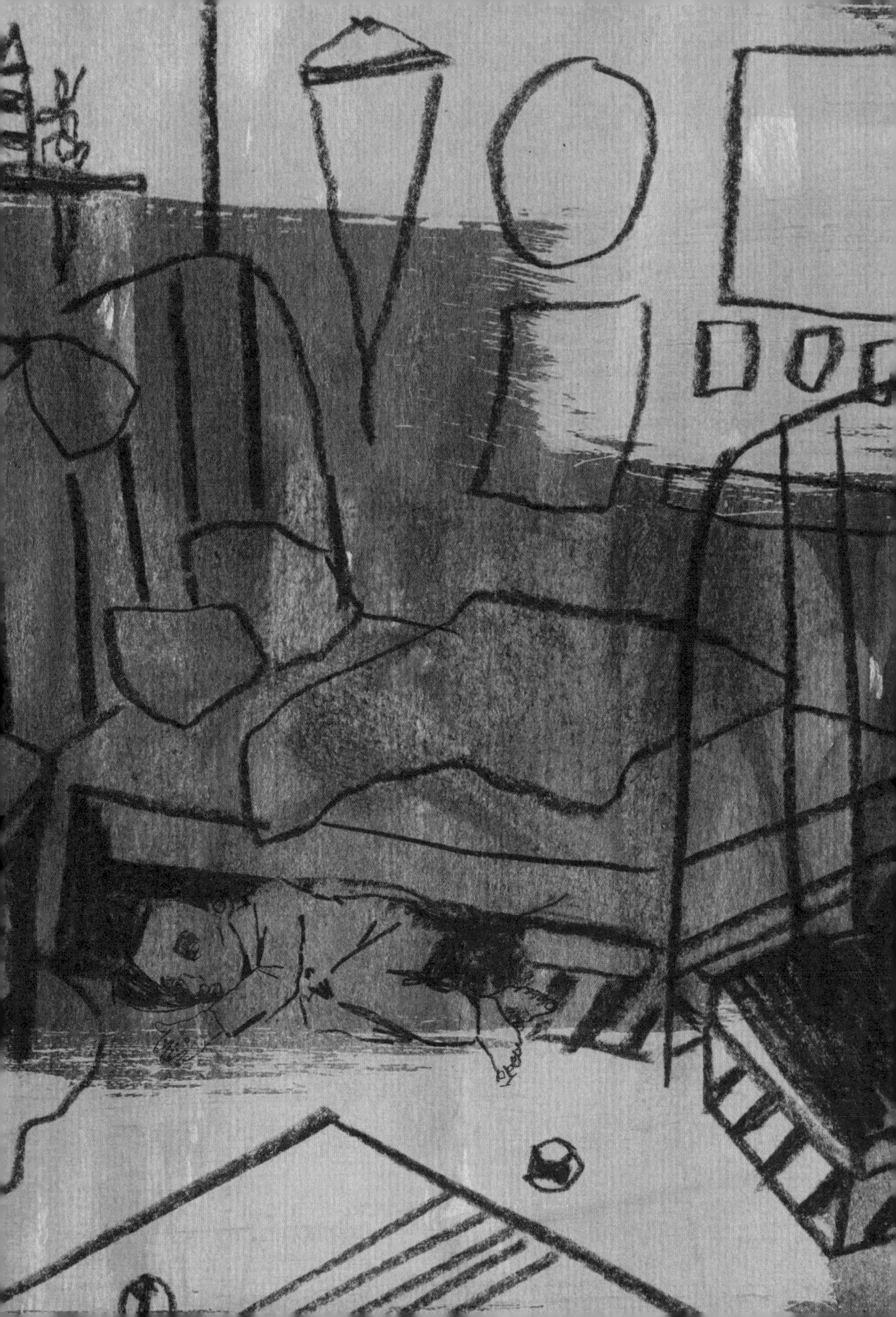
DO

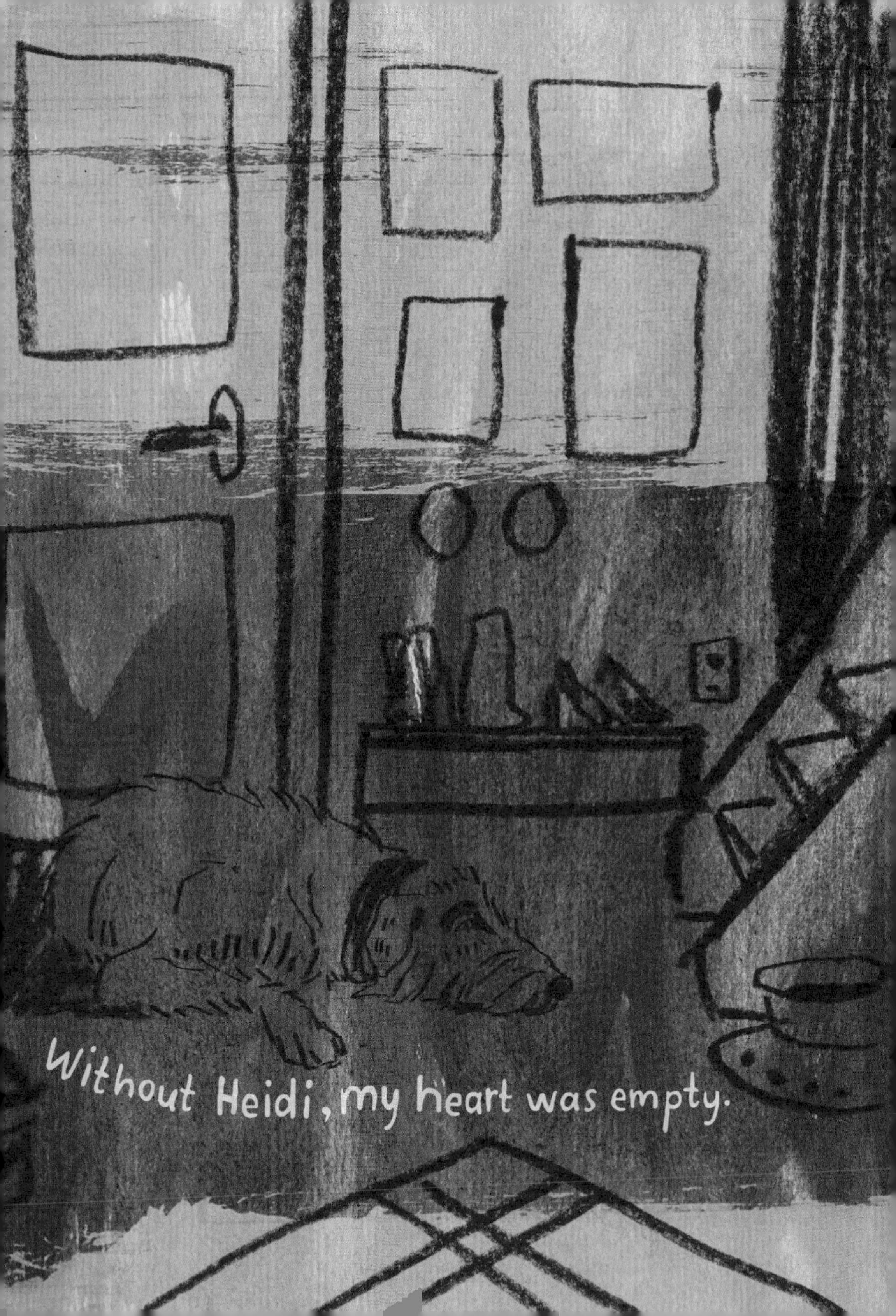
Without Heidi, my heart was empty.

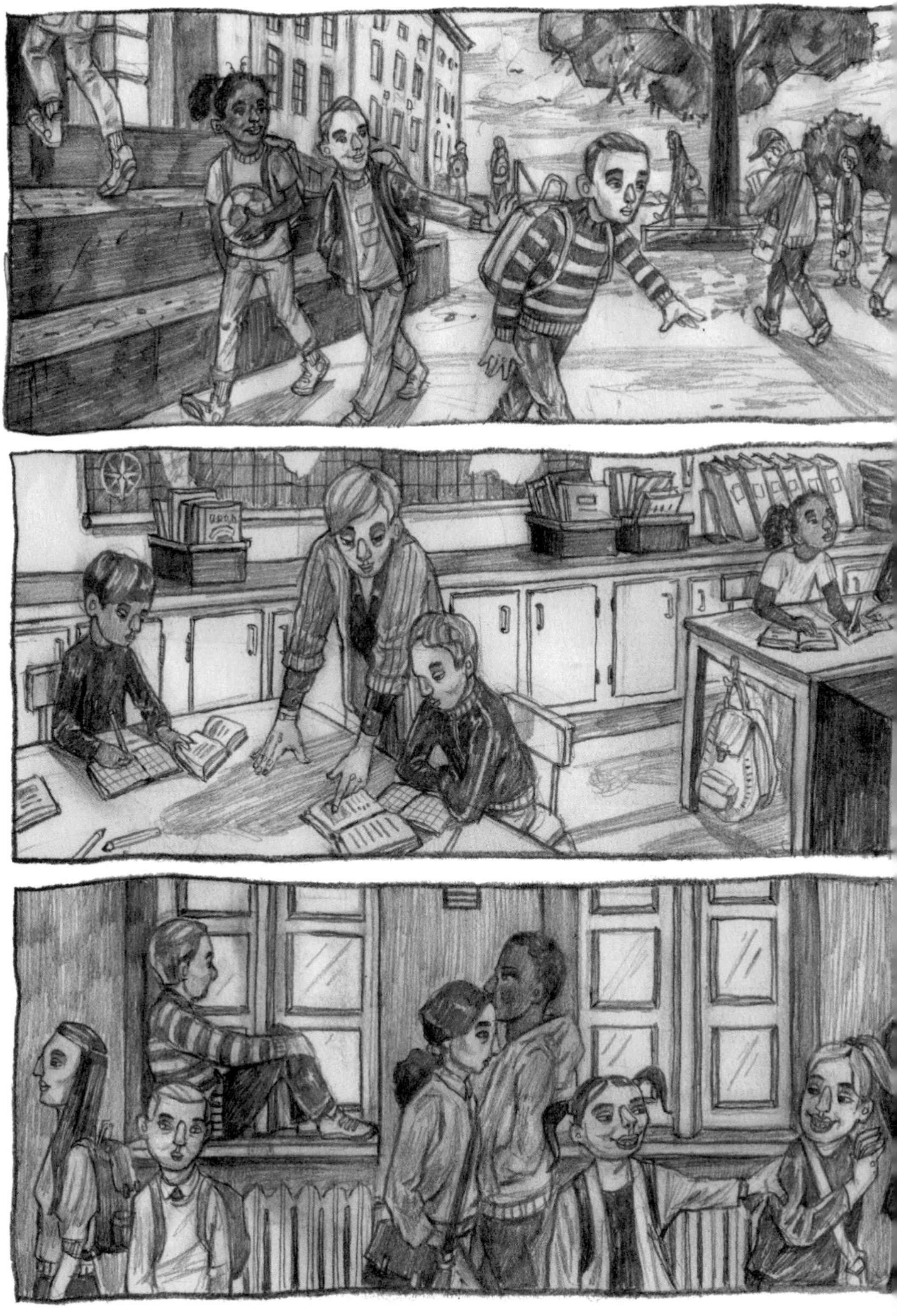

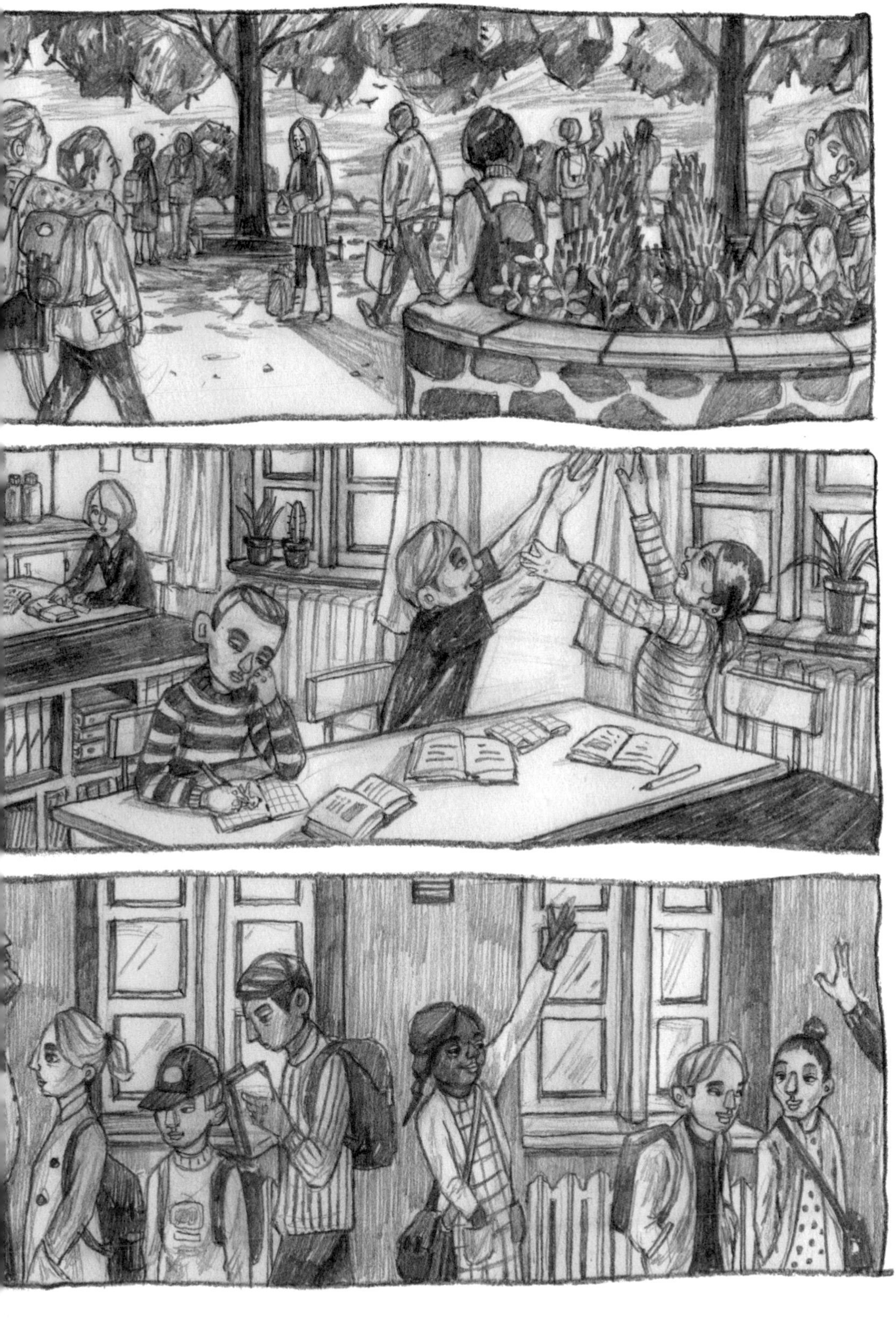

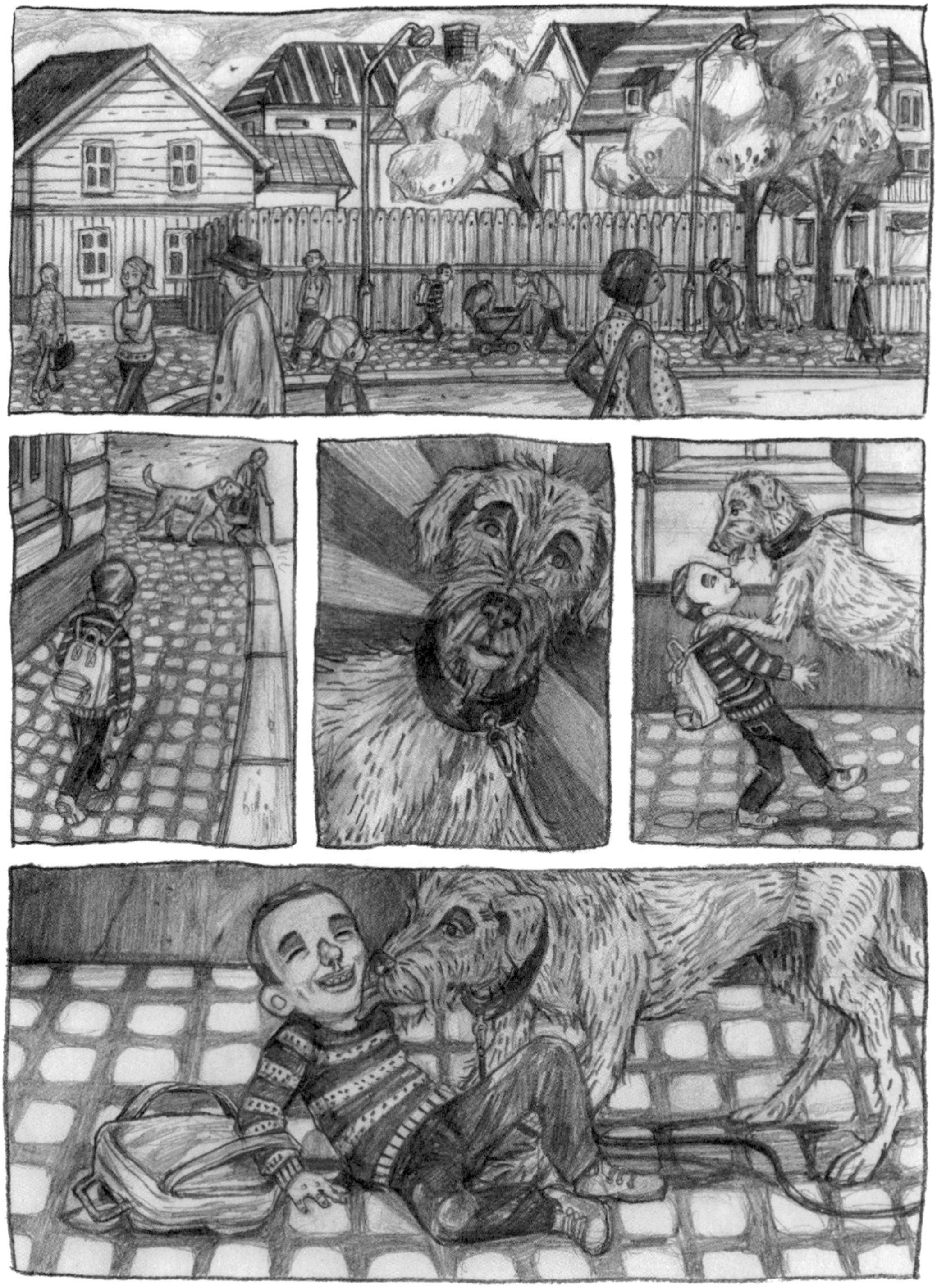

One day we found each other again. How lucky!

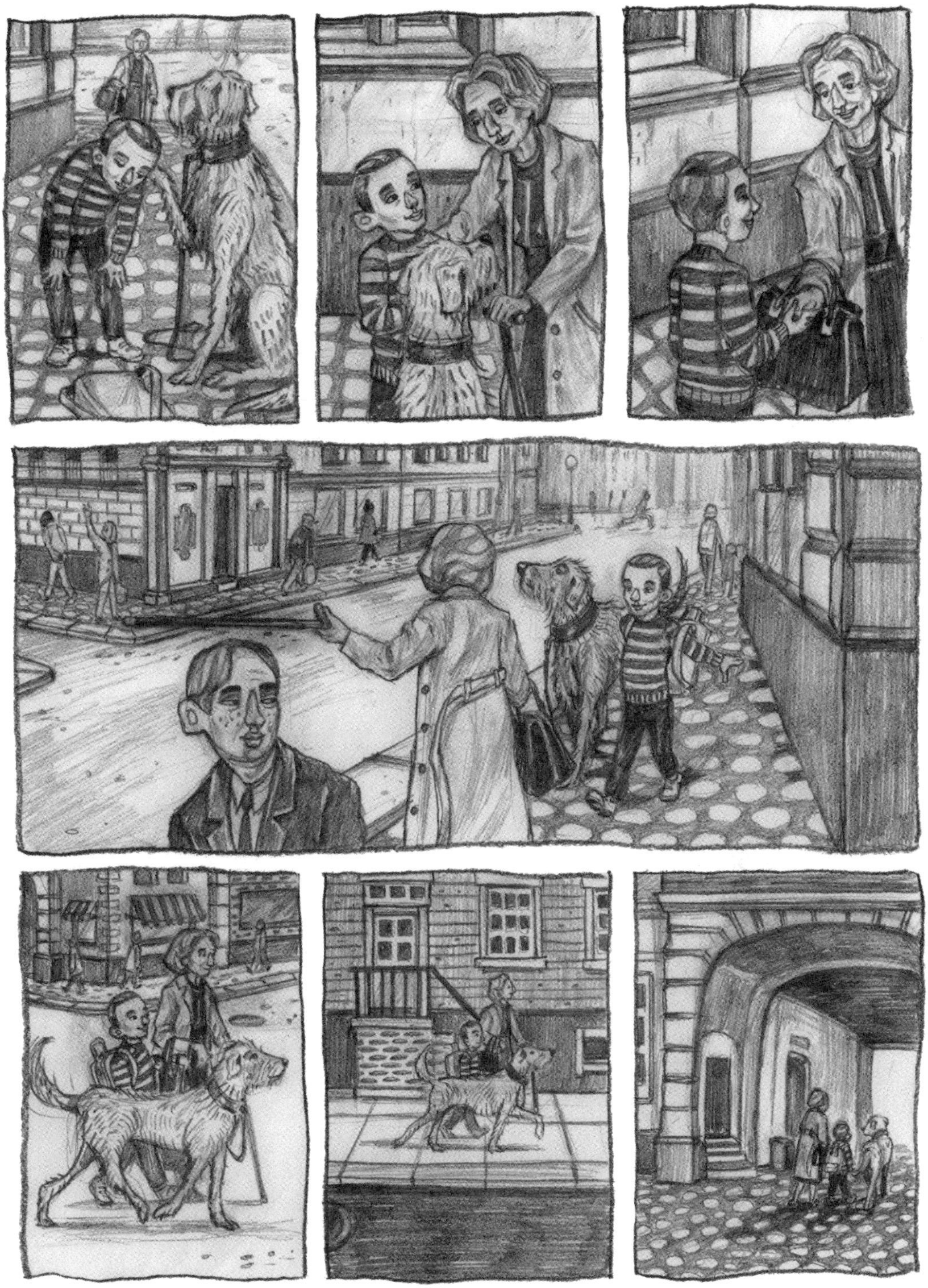

The lady was nice.

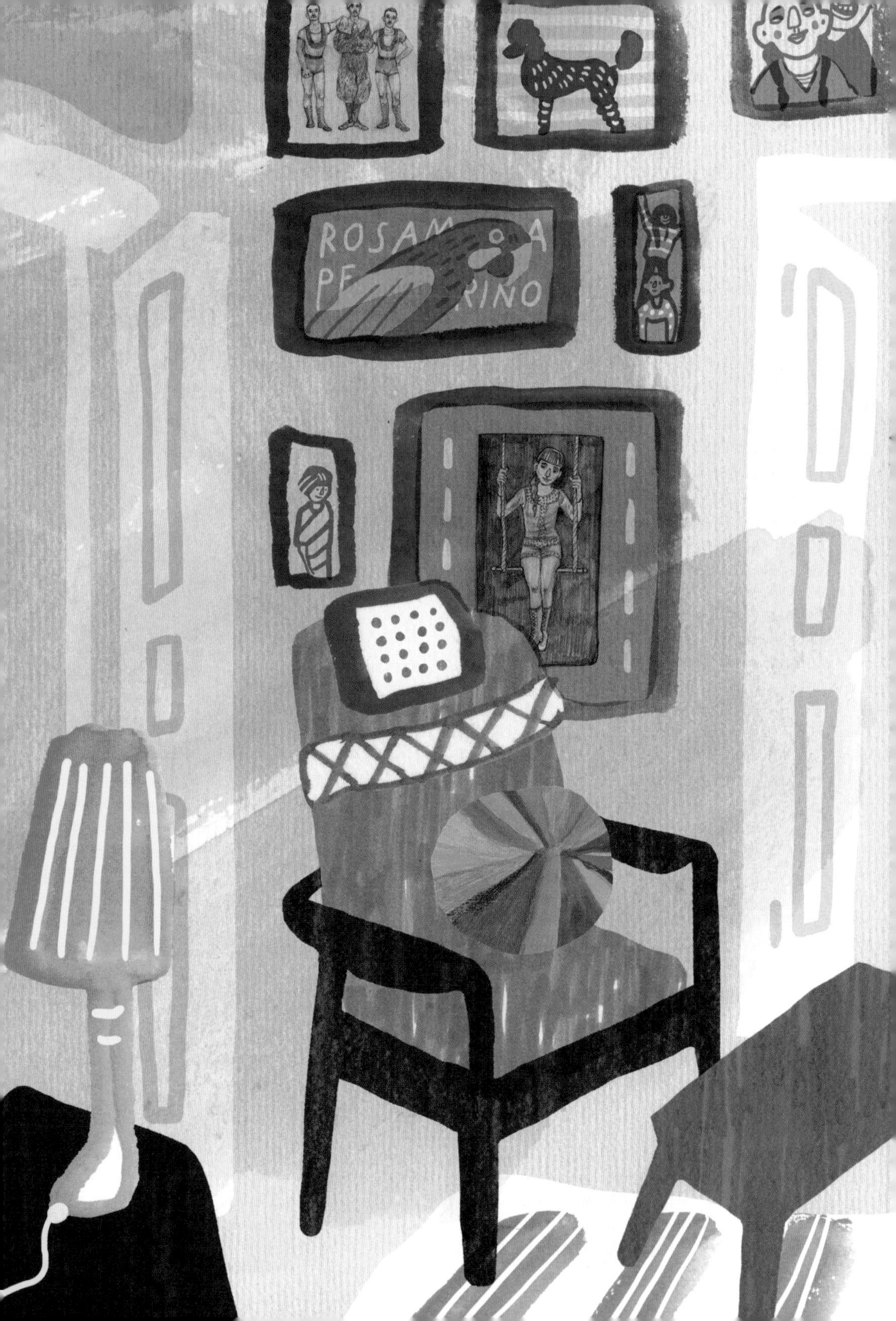
ROSAM A
PE RINO

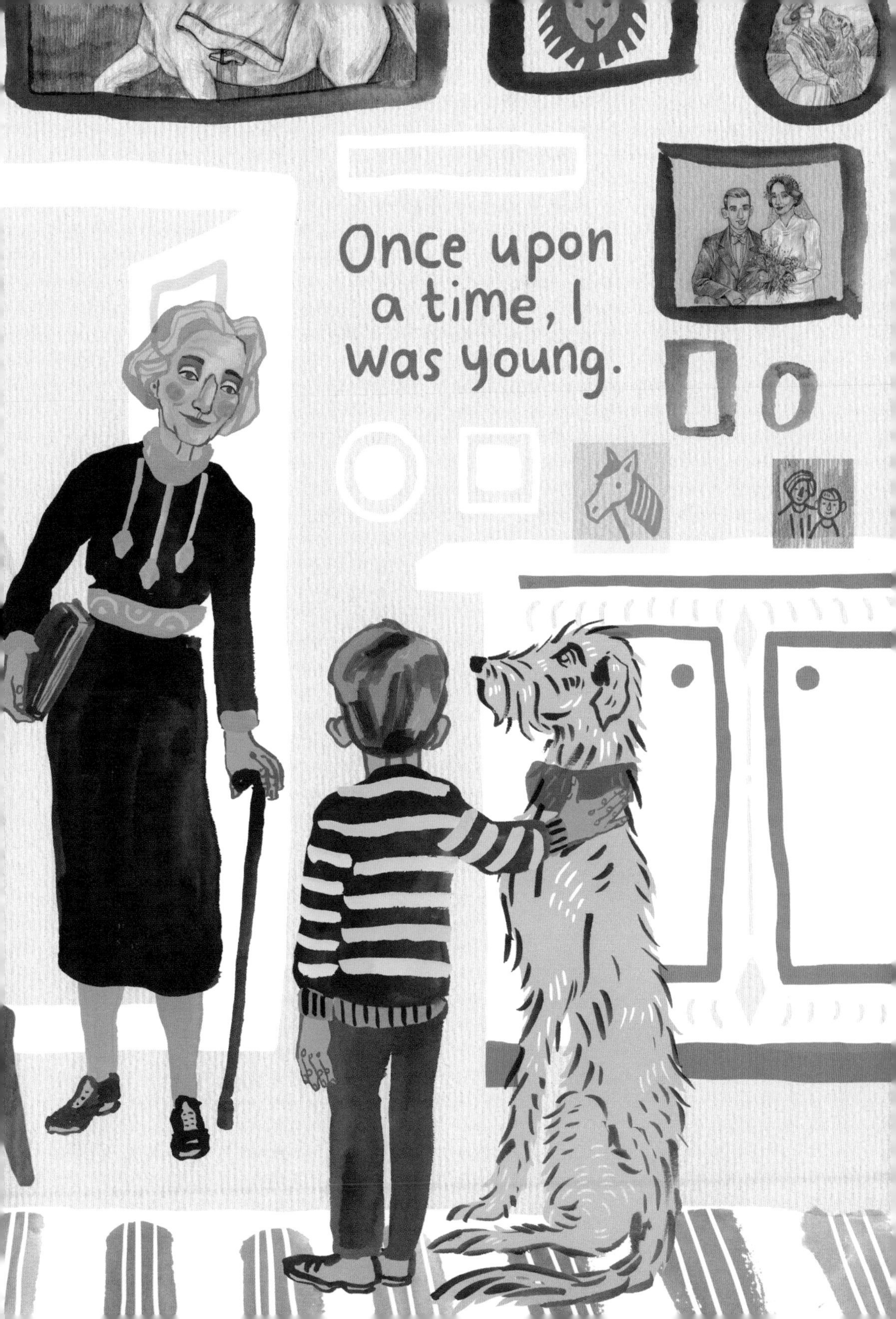

Once upon a time, I was young.

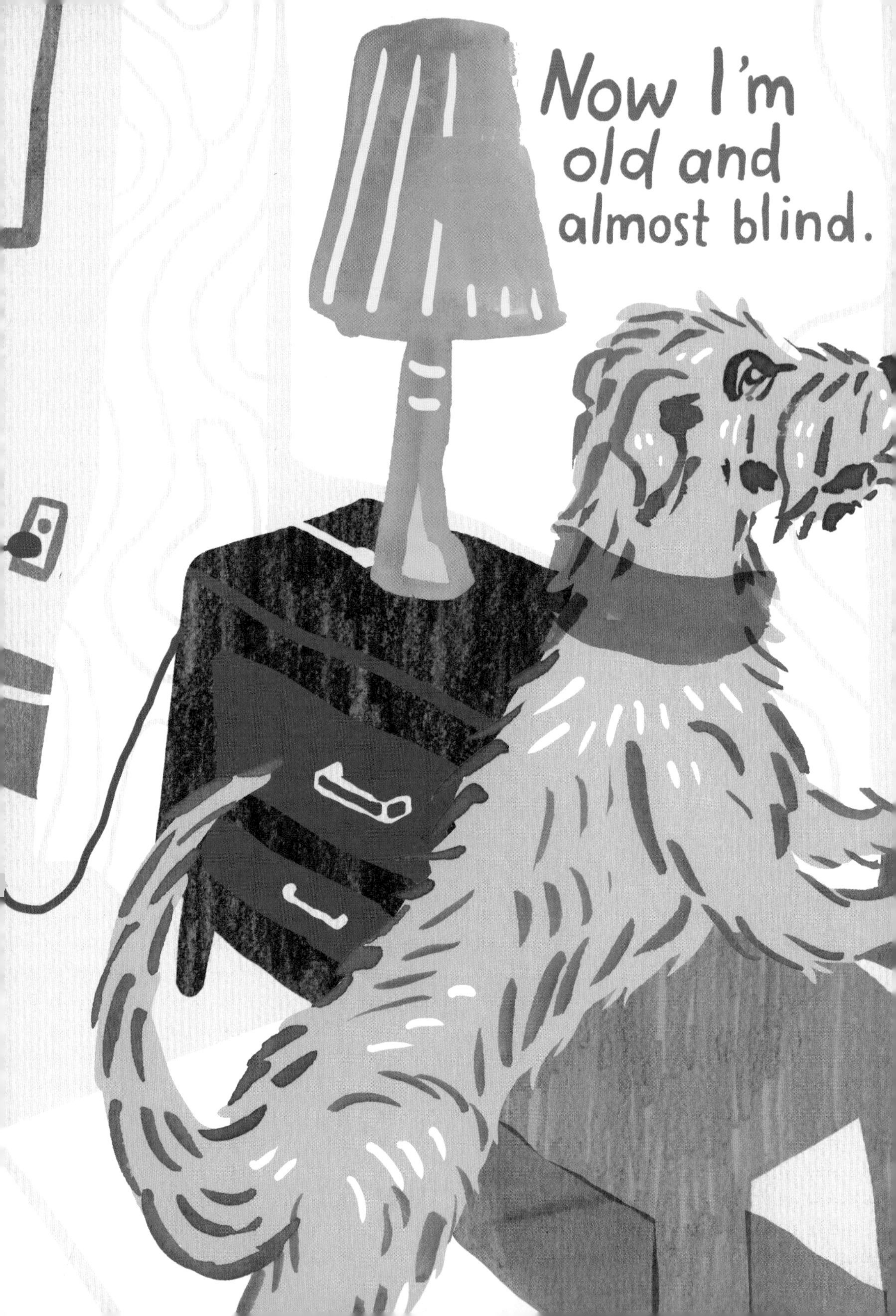
Now I'm old and almost blind.

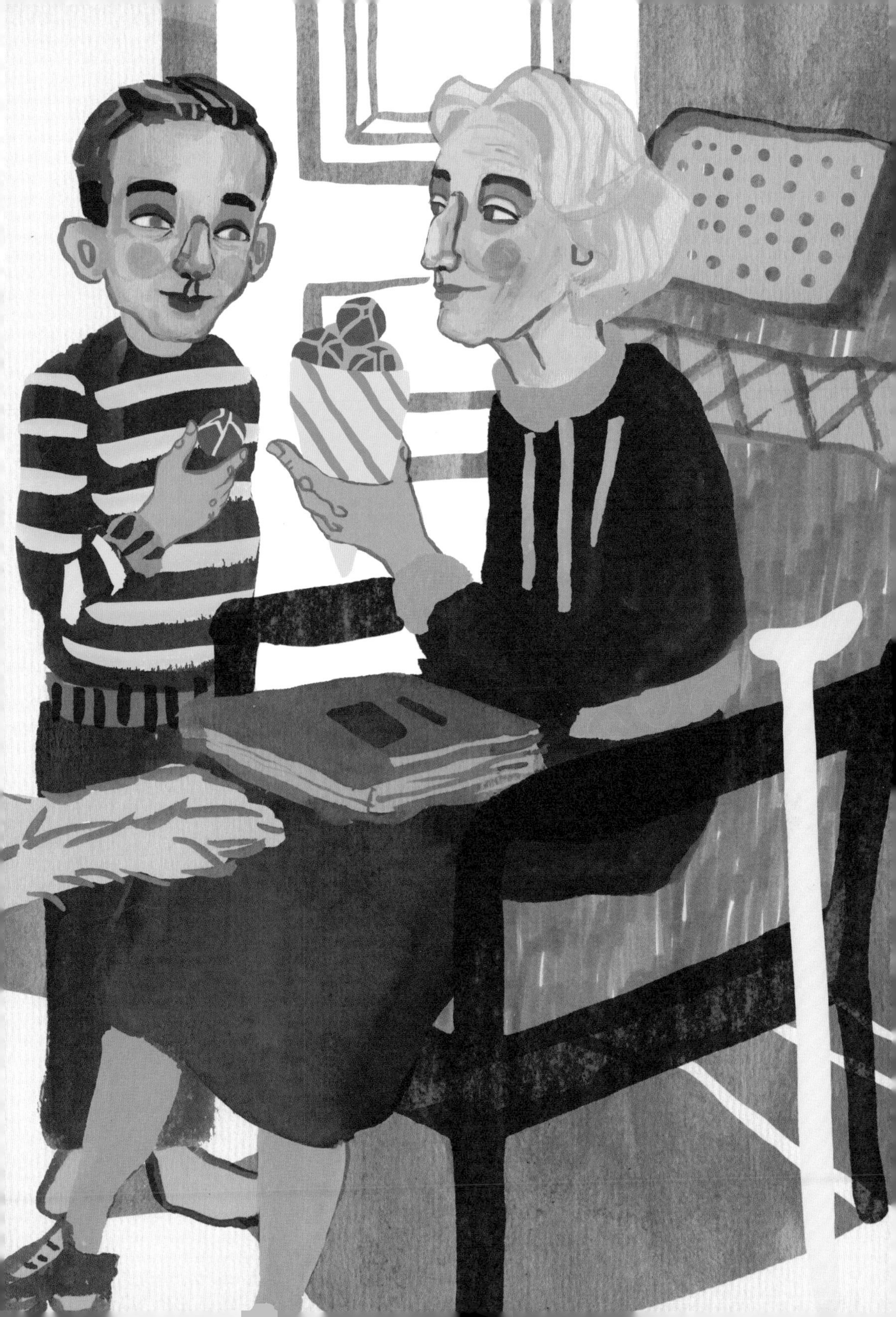

I can read to you.

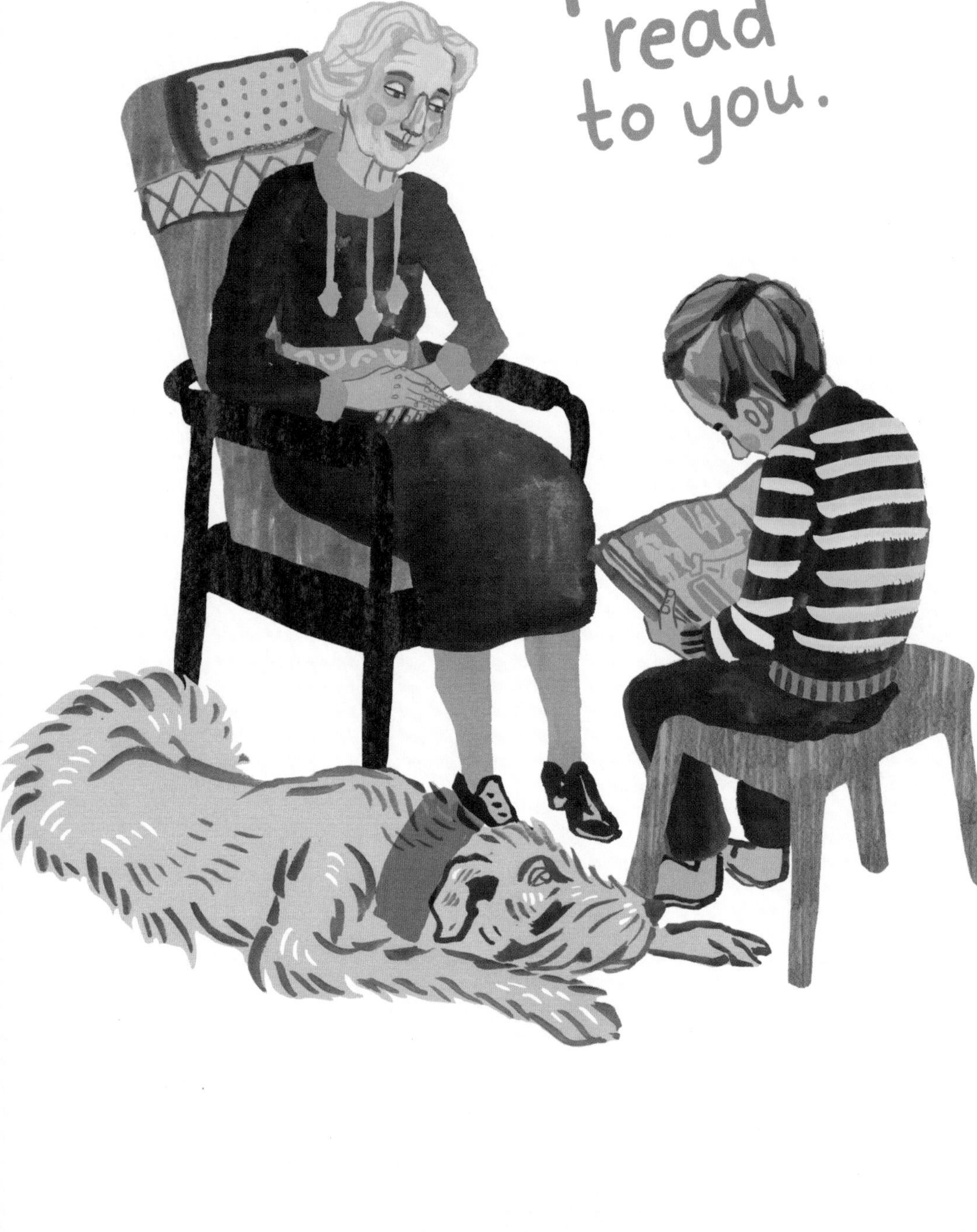

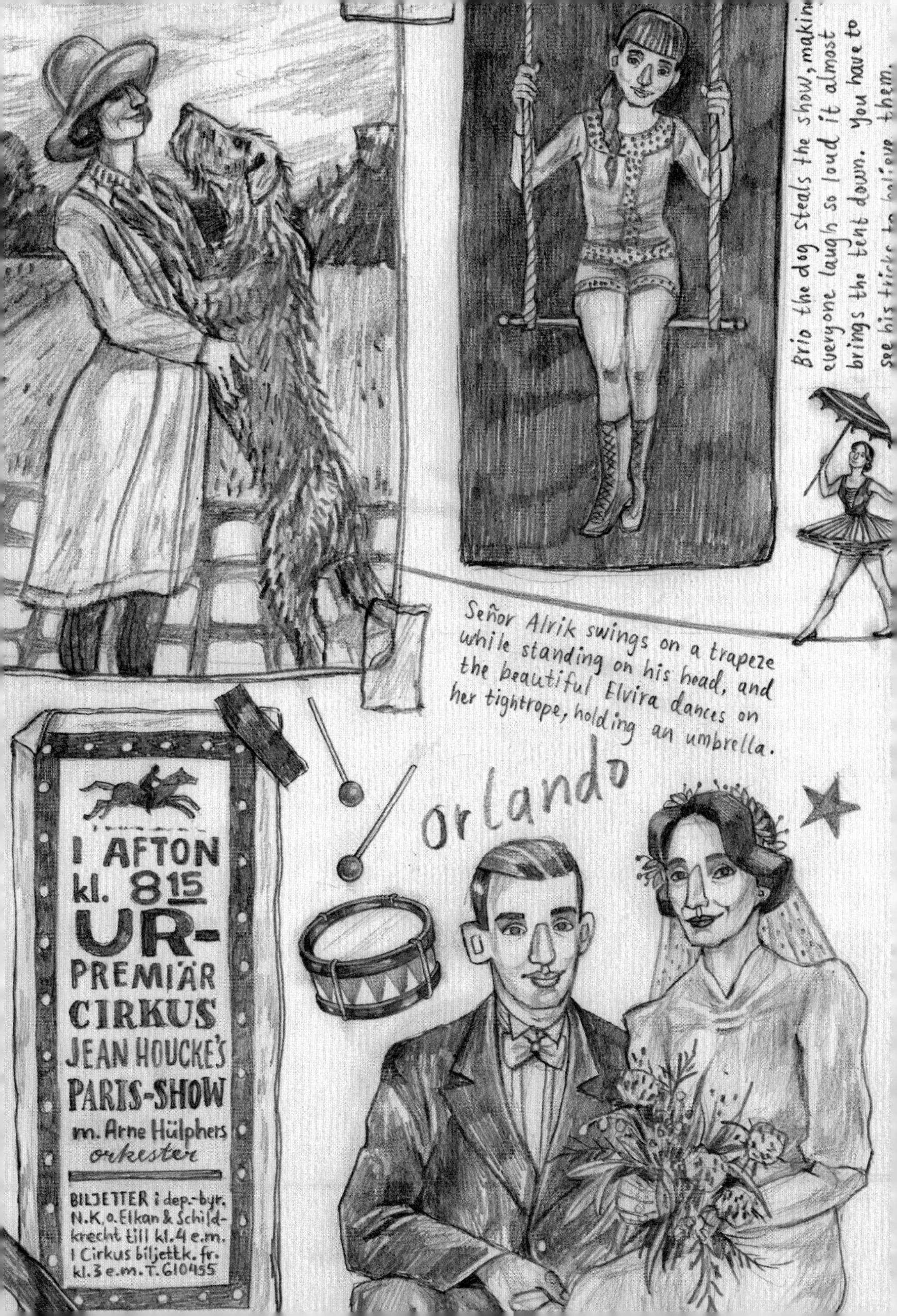
Brio the dog steals the show, makin
everyone laugh so loud it almost
brings the tent down. You have to
see his tricks to believe them.
Señor Alrik swings on a trapeze
while standing on his head, and
the beautiful Elvira dances on
her tightrope, holding an umbrella.
Orlando
I AFTON
kl. 8 15
UR-
PREMIÄR
CIRKUS
JEAN HOUCKE'S
PARIS-SHOW
m. Arne Hülphers
orkester
BILJETTER i dep.-byr.
N.K. o. Elkan & Schildkrecht till kl. 4 e.m.
I Cirkus biljettk. fr.
kl. 3 e.m. T. 610455

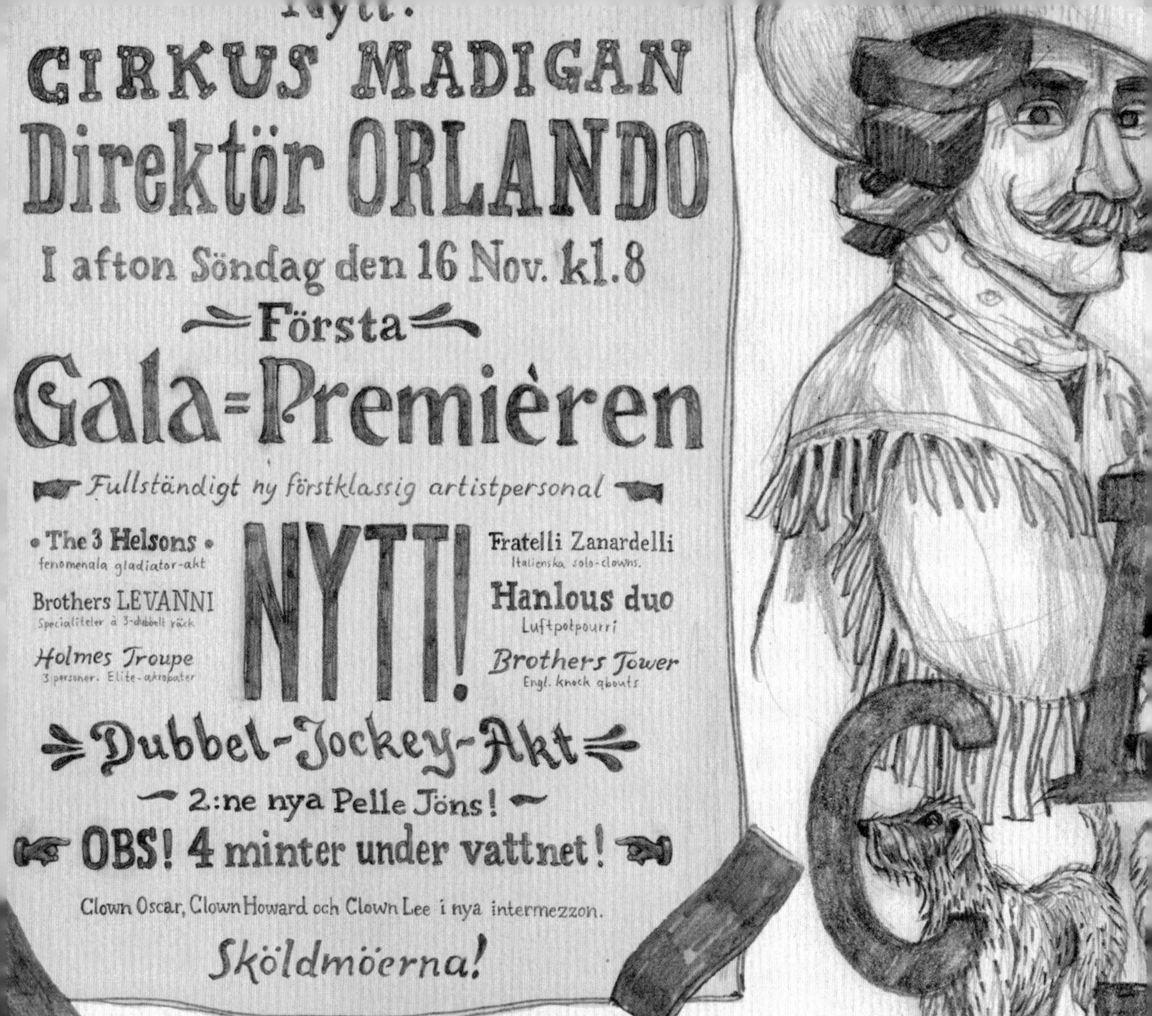
CIRKUS MADIGAN
Direktör ORLANDO
I afton Söndag den 16 Nov. kl.8
Första
Gala=Premièren
Fullständigt ny förstklassig artistpersonal
The 3 Helsons
fenomenala gladiator-akt
Brothers LEVANNI
Specialiteter à 3-dubbelt räck
Holmes Troupe
3 personer. Elite-akrobater
NYTT!
Fratelli Zanardelli
Italienska solo-clowns.
Hanlous duo
Luftpotpourri
Brothers Tower
Engl. knock abouts
Dubbel-Jockey-Akt
2:ne nya Pelle Jöns!
OBS! 4 minter under vattnet!
Clown Oscar, Clown Howard och Clown Lee i nya intermezzon.
Sköldmöerna!

A raging fire broke out last night in one of the circus cars near Södra Esplanaden. It looked like the fire might spread to the circus tent and the rest of the cars, but the firefighters arrived quickly.

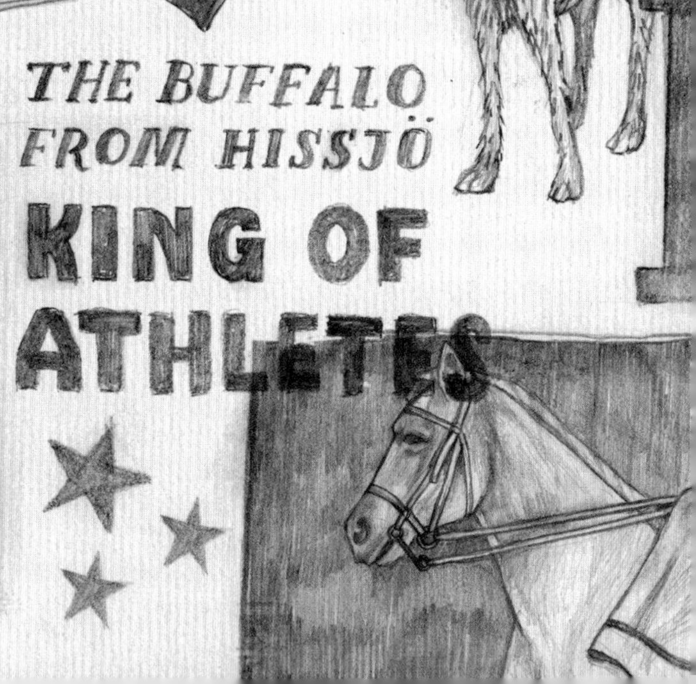
THE BUFFALO
FROM HISSJÖ
KING OF
ATHLETES